Book Two of

The Emergence

of the

Shaman

E . W . FARNSWORTH

Book Two of the Wiglaff Chronicles

The
Emergence
of the
Shaman

E. W. FARNSWORTH

ZIMBELL HOUSE
PUBLISHING
UNION LAKE, MICHIGAN

For permission requests, write to the publisher at the address below:
"Attention: Permissions Coordinator"
Zimbell House Publishing, LLC
PO Box 1172
Union Lake, Michigan 48387
mail to: info@zimbellhousepublishing.com

© 2017 E. W. Farnsworth
Book and Cover Design by The Book Planners
http://www.TheBookPlanner.com

Published in the United States by Zimbell House Publishing
http://www.ZimbellHousePublishing.com
All Rights Reserved

Trade Paper ISBN: 978-1945967238
Kindle ISBN: 978-1945967245
Digital ISBN: 978-1945967252
Library of Congress Control Number: 2017905168

First Edition: May/2017
10 9 8 7 6 5 4 3 2 1

DEDICATION

For Ev

CONTENTS

FOREWORD

"Scotland during the Roman Empire refers to the protohistorical period during which the Roman Empire interacted with the area that is now Scotland, which was known to them as "Caledonia". Roman legions arrived around AD 71, having conquered the Celtic tribes of "Britain" (England and Wales) over the preceding three decades. Aiming to annex all of the island of "Albion", Romans under Q. Petilius Cerialis and Gn. Julius Agricola invaded the Caledonians in the 70s and 80s. An account by Agricola's son-in-law Tacitus mentions a Roman victory at "Mons Graupius" which became the namesake of the Grampians but has been questioned by modern scholarship. The Romans then seem to have repeated an earlier Greek circumnavigation of the island and received submission from local tribes, establishing their border of actual control first along the Gask Ridge before withdrawing to a line south of the Solway Firth. This line was fortified as Hadrian's Wall. Several Roman commanders attempted to fully conquer lands north of this line, including a brief expansion that was fortified as the Antonine Wall. Despite grandiose claims made by an 18th-century forged manuscript, however, it is now believed that the Romans at no point controlled even half of present-day Scotland and that Roman legions ceased to affect the area after around 211.

The history of the period is complex and not well-documented. The province of Valentia, for instance, may have been the lands between the two Roman walls, or the territory around and south of Hadrian's Wall, or Roman Wales. Romans held most of their Caledonian territory only a little over 40 years; they probably only held any Scottish land at all for about 80 years. Some Scottish historians such as Moffat go so far as to say Rome's presence was entirely uninfluential. "Scots" and "Scotland" proper would not emerge as unified ideas until centuries later. In fact, the Roman

*Empire influenced every part of Scotland during the period: by the time of the Roman withdrawal from Britain around 410, the various Iron Age tribes native to the area had united as or fell under the control of the Picts while the southern half of the country was overrun by tribes of Romanized Britons. The Scoti, **Gaelic** Irish raiders who would give Scotland its English name, had begun to settle along the west coast as well. All three groups may have been involved in the Great Conspiracy that overran Roman Britain in 367. The era also saw the emergence of the earliest historical accounts of the natives. The most enduring legacies of Rome, however, were Christianity and literacy, both of which arrived indirectly via Irish missionaries."*

— https://en.wikipedia.org/wiki/Scotland_during_the_Roman_Empire

Chapter One

Wiglaff the Beginning

"Genius is distinguished from talent, both quantitatively and qualitatively. Talent refers to a native aptitude for some special kind of work and implies a relatively quick and easy acquisition of a particular skill within a domain (sphere of activity or knowledge). Genius, on the other hand, involves originality, creativity, and the ability to think and work in areas not previously explored—thus giving the world something of value that would not otherwise exist."
—Barbara Kerr, "Genius Psychology," Encyclopaedia Britannica

WIGLAFF knew he did not belong. He was different from his siblings and the villagers in every respect. His father, the great warrior Mordru, was disgusted by his eldest son's aversion to war and the way he communed with nature. His mother, Onna, worried her husband would take her beloved son into the forest and either lose or kill him. The boy had survived through eleven frigid winters. This twelfth winter promised to be snowy and extremely cold. Wooly bears had worn thick black summer coats; such signs could not be ignored.

Everyone agreed that the boy had gifts for listening and observing. He was the first to hear a rabbit making its way through the snow. He knew the different spiders by the design of their webs. When a forest fire threatened, his nose would twitch with the first scent of smoke in the air. He would announce the fire in a song he invented, "Fire, smoke in empty air. It comes from there." He would incline his head and point in the direction where the fire was starting. He was never wrong.

Wiglaff also played with animals, for which he was no threat. Whether a spring fawn or a ferocious bear or wolf, the boy would find ways to approach and pet the beasts and feed them from his gentle, graceful hands. When his father decided to use him as a lure for game, for a while, Wiglaff ceased his practice of communing with animals. This infuriated the clansmen who saw no use in a dreamer who would not contribute to the common welfare. He became the butt of vicious jokes that only stopped when the boy's artistry at making sure weapons became known.

Even at this early age, Wiglaff was adept at telling poisonous toadstools from edible mushrooms. Others would bring him baskets of gathered spores, and he would sort them infallibly. Some of the poisonous ones he kept for special purposes only known to himself. As for forest plants, he knew the poison ivy, oak, and sumac and avoided them. He could find a succulent root using his nose and fingers in the damp, black soil. Like a skunk, he could find fat grubs and insects crawling just below the mosses. Seeds and nuts were his special daily harvests; the types depended upon the season. He filled sacks for use in winter, when the dried meats and fruits would run out.

Surprising to say, the boy did not require teaching. This disturbed his fellow villagers more than his other foibles. The villagers could be heard grumbling amongst themselves about the sources of his unique knowledge, and why no one else had been given the privilege of knowing what the boy seemed to know instinctively. The women were jealous, especially the witches and sorceresses. They felt the boy trespassed on their sacred domains. The more they studied the boy, though, the more they were impressed. They adopted his methods where they could. When he snuck through the woods on a rainy night, they followed him. He would disappear for a while in summer months; then he would come to them with giant bullfrogs croaking in each hand.

Wiglaff's mother, Onna, worried most when her son went into his trances. His eyes would take on a faraway look. His breath would be so shallow she feared he was dead or dying. Relaxing with his hands open except with his index fingers touching on his thumbs, he was deaf to all her questions and insensitive to her touch.

Winna, his sister, was enlisted by his mother to watch over her brother. She resented this job at first because she felt she was as much a warrior as her father and detested weakness in men. Yet she was a female and therefore, thought to be inferior. Even though she felt constrained with the job of babysitting her elder brother, she took the task imposed by her mother to improve her own skills of seeing and protecting.

With Autumn came the increasingly colder daily rains. It also brought seeds and vibrant colors in the foliage. Caledonia became a red and gold tapestry of trees, with evergreens piercing through as a reminder of other seasons that lay on either side of winter. With fall also came hibernation and the emergence of creatures that practiced aestivation.

Chilly weather did not seem to affect Wiglaff, though snot ran through his nose and constantly dripped as did everyone else's in his village. Where the others were perpetually hungry and eating all the time, the boy Wiglaff had the advantage of requiring little food. He had no fat on his body, but he gained energy from drinking water from icy streams or from tickling trout whose flesh he ate raw after studying the red speckles on their light brown skin and the red fans of their gills.

One blessing from his mother's viewpoint was his inerrant ability to find honeycombs by tracing bees to their hives. Others paid no attention to the insects preparing for the harsh winter. Wiglaff studied the paths of bees and by means known only to him, was able to find the hollow trees and stumps where the golden honey streamed. He also knew how to harvest combs of dripping nectar without apparently being stung by the guardians of the hives.

Onna would often be surprised by her son, surrounded by honeybees, showing up at their hut's opening with combs in both his tiny hands and honey dripping on the ground. She had a special container for these gifts, which was filled during the season and provided a binder for bags of seeds that Wiglaff also harvested during autumn.

Wiglaff's father, Mordru, grudgingly acknowledged his son's harvest contributions but complained he might also track and kill animals like rabbits, rats, and squirrels. The boy was not squeamish about killing game, but he had no interest in butchering meat. Instead, he communed with the others' prey. Further, when hunters cleared animals for food, Wiglaff's father was disturbed by what his son did with the remains.

Observing how her brother killed those animals for his private purposes, Winna noticed that he would inspect their entrails and eat the hearts and livers, and sometimes the vertebrae. One time she saw him pick up a giant rat by the tail, hold the tail while the rat pulled against him and lower a pointed rock on the back of the animal's neck. Wiglaff skinned the rat deftly, setting aside its pelt. He beckoned his watcher and gave her the flesh while he reserved the innards for himself.

Winna wondered about her brother and often asked him in private why he did the strange things that set him apart from her and the others. On days when he felt like talking about it, he told her he was compelled by forces within him.

On days when he felt like being silent, he was deaf to her entreaties.

He knew she resented having to watch him, and he told her he sympathized, "Winna since you resent having to watch what I do, why do you do it?" He seemed genuinely interested in her motivation.

"I do what I'm told. Mother would beat me if I didn't follow you and report what you were doing. If you were in my place, what would you do?" she asked with raised eyebrows.

Wiglaff did not answer her question. Instead, he rolled his eyes and offered her the pelts from the rats he had slain for his ceremonies, not to dissuade her from watching him, but to show her he meant no harm by asking his question. "You know, you're as strange as I am in your own way. I don't tell on you when you train like men with your girlfriends. I know when you sneak out at night to drill as if you were warriors."

Winna winced, "Okay. But I have found a mission to help our villagers with my talents. What have you done? When our enemies attack, will you be cowering in the woods or fighting?"

The other village boys taunted Wiglaff tirelessly. They called him names, like coward, dreamer, and crazy. Wiglaff pretended not to hear them. When they got rough and shoved him, Winna stepped between her brother and the bullies. They learned not to tangle with Wiglaff's sister. When she took offense, she never forgot why she did so.

Winna's ability to win a fight against even the strongest village boys became a legend. A few large, strong boys decided they would gang up on her, but she defeated them all by stealthy means. Those would-be-warriors never forgot the lesson: "Don't ever tangle with Winna!"

Her father laughed when he heard how his daughter defended her brother. Wiglaff might be considered an imbecile and coward, but Winna was everything Mordru had wished in his son. Grudgingly he began letting her train as a warrior, while purposely excluding his son and supposed heir from the privilege. Mordru set Wiglaff to carving shafts for arrows and spears or handles for clubs and axes, for the village arsenal. To these, the boy attached wet strips of leather, fastened flint, and other hard stones he had found and chipped to sharpness.

Training for war was constant because Caledonia was always at war. Village raided and fought against village; tribe preyed on tribe; clan warred against clan. Even within families, jealousy and spite divided all parties. No one seemed to agree with anyone else. For Wiglaff's parents, Mordru and Onna, this was not an unjust or unusual situation; it was the way things always had been. Wiglaff had not experienced war outside his nuclear family until his twelfth winter. Because game was scarce, and nature had not been as bountiful as usual with nuts and fruits, one village raided another. Most often, raids involved theft of stores, weapons, and small damage to property. Sometimes, though, villagers were injured. Sometimes villagers were even killed; men, women, and children.

Wiglaff was deep in the forest when the raid began. He heard a great commotion and fell to the forest floor, crawling into sough that covered him. He hid and watched from where he lay. He saw the members of the raiding party and memorized the features of each man. He heard their names as they addressed one another. When the raiders departed with their plunder, he followed them stealthily and heard their remarks to each other about another planned raid against his village.

That evening when Wiglaff returned to his hut for his dinner, he listened to his father and sister discussing the raid in cryptic terms. His father waved his hands and threatened to find, track and kill the robbers. Winna seconded his plan, gripping her hands into fists, her eyes flashing defiance and death to the enemy villagers.

Onna's eyes scanned her family, and asked, "Wiglaff what do you think?"

Lowering his eyes, the boy mumbled the names of the raiders. He said, "I followed them to their village and heard them talk about their plan for a second raid on the village tomorrow night."

Mordru narrowed his eyes, "Are you sure of what you're saying?"

"Yes, Father."

Mordru looked doubtful and turned to Winna for confirmation.

Winna stood tall as she defended her brother saying, "Father, if Wiglaff says it's so, believe him. I do."

Both Mordru and Winna were astonished by the waif's intelligence and initiative. They asked a dozen questions wanting to know where he hid when he heard the raiders planning, how many total raiders were involved, the name of their leader, the weapons they carried, and so forth. Wiglaff answered all their questions clearly without hesitation.

"If you were a warrior, you would have attacked the raiders and taught them a lesson they'd never forget." Mordru scoffed.

Onna came to Wiglaff's defense. "Is it wise for a single unarmed boy to attack a dozen fully armed raiders? I don't think so." Turning to Wiglaff, she asked, "Will you lead a band of our men to the place where they can teach these outlaws not to underestimate us?"

Wiglaff thought for a moment and told Mordru and Winna, "I volunteer to lead you and a dozen of our men to the raiders' village."

***

Early the next morning, Wiglaff, with Winna at his side, led Mordru's troops to the village where the raiders were dividing up their spoils, right in the village square. Rushing by the boy and his sister, Mordru and his men slew the raiders and took back their stores as well as the supplies and weapons of the raiders' village. They burned the raiders' huts to the ground and left the women and children weeping and vowing revenge.

Wiglaff and Winna did not realize it at the time, but Mordru made this counter-raid his method of retaliating against all marauders. Winna was so impressed by her brother's acumen, she decided to become a silent tracker and to school herself off her brother's skills of observation. She had the warrior's impatience, where Wiglaff had no sense of urgency at all. Because Wiglaff loved his pesky sister in spite of her constant tattling on him, he cautioned her how to track silently, how to read forest signs and how to remain unobserved.

Wiglaff became the eyes and ears of his village that winter. He understood his role and stayed out late each night watching for new trouble. When snow fell, he let it cover him so he could watch from a snowdrift unobserved. The silence of snow allowed him to hear the sounds of men moving through the forest. If they moved toward another village, Wiglaff took no notice. If the noises indicated a threat to his own community, he would withdraw quickly and silently to raise the alarm.

Sometimes Winna would watch alongside him. When there was something to report, he would then send her running to their father. While she ran through the woods, Wiglaff continued to watch the raiders.

Wiglaff's father, Mordru, was so effective dealing with the thieves, they wondered what special powers he employed to gain an advantage. To the raiders, children like Wiglaff and Winna did not figure in their thoughts, so they never could discover that the secret was the young brother and sister working as a team.

One raiding party walking through the snow happened on Wiglaff's hiding place. They found the boy playing with twigs and leaves. He had caught a vole and placed it in a cage of woven wood and bark. The raiders laughed and jostled the boy before they continued toward the village on their marauding venture. Winna, who was hiding a short distance from Wiglaff at that time, sprinted to the village to raise the alarm. Meanwhile, Wiglaff followed by moonlight the trail the raiders had left in the snow. He used their footsteps to mask his own. In this way, he discovered how the raiders had skirted a neighboring village to lay blame on others for their deeds.

Returning to his village, Wiglaff found Mordru in a council of war to retaliate against the community which had sent the raiders. Knowing his father would not like hearing the truth, Wiglaff told Onna and Winna what he had learned about the raiders' origin. Onna took this information to her husband, but Mordru was already convinced the neighboring village had attacked. He would not listen to the facts and had no time to listen to his worthless son.

The result of Mordru's hot-headed determination was that his attack on the innocent village the raiders had intended to use as scapegoats, was ultimately used as a lesson to anyone else planning to steal from his village. Meanwhile, the real raiders sat calmly in their own village square dividing their spoils while the attack ensued. Wiglaff's father only realized his mistake when no evidence of the spoils was found in the village his men attacked. He ordered the village burned to the ground even though its villagers were not to blame.

When truth is not the basis for war, errors compound swiftly. The actual raiders forged an alliance of communities to punish the marauders from Mordru's village. Though it was a time of ice, wind and freezing rain, the multi-village attack against Mordru's village came soon thereafter. Wiglaff's father and his men did a creditable job defending themselves, but some brave warriors died.

With her spear, Winna made her first kill of a raider who was about to hack down her father from behind. This taste of death made her proud and sealed the young girl's fate as a future warrior. Her father never forgot her action. Afterward, though, he could never acknowledge what had happened. Mordru's esteem would have diminished among his male warriors if it became generally known that his life had been saved from death by a mere girl.

Having defeated an alliance of communities, Mordru's village ironically became even more vulnerable than before. The opposing alliance of communities grew. This, in turn, caused Mordru's village to form partnerships of its own. Wiglaff realized the import of the coming war. He did his part by fashioning the weapons, and he spent part of his day in seclusion to discover how else he could assist his fellow villagers. Winna followed her brother into his seclusion and sat nearby while he did strange things she did not understand.

Going into a trance, Wiglaff murmured to himself while he held out his hands, palms upward. He fetched out his captive vole from its cage. He sacrificed it with one of his sharp flint knives. Flaying the tiny corpse, he chopped the neck and crunched the vertebrae between his teeth. He then cut out the heart and liver and ate them. Looking upward, he made a cawing sound. A crow descended and landed on the ground in front of him. From Wiglaff's hand, the crow ate pieces of vole meat. It then began to talk with Wiglaff, who answered, cawing as if the two understood each other perfectly. Winna sat captivated by what she saw but remained silent to witness her brother's methods.

When the crow took off, Wiglaff came out of his trance and cleaned up the area where he had conducted the sacrifice of the vole. Winna took this opportunity to ask him questions.

"Brother, a crow came and talked with you. What did you say to each other?"

Wiglaff nodded. His eyes focused on hers. "The crow and I discussed the information I needed."

Winna shook her head. She was not satisfied with his answer. "What information did you request?"

"I told him to gather his fellow crows and fly to each village for a day's march in all directions to discover which villages were friendly to ours and which were allied against us."

She frowned. "And you think the crow will return with the information you want?"

Wiglaff fixed his gaze on her and asked her, "Why shouldn't the crow do that?"

Winna laughed and stood up to shake her arms and stretch her legs. "When do you expect the crow to return?"

Her brother shrugged. "Maybe the crow won't return, after all. Of all birds, it's the only one that recognizes me in a crowd. One day it flew onto my shoulder and cawed for food. Since then it has taken me a long while to earn the trust of this bird. I don't expect you to believe me. I'm going to build a small fire. Would you like me to make you a pair of vole skin gloves? I can keep the fur on or shave it off. If you want to wear the gloves when you wield weapons, you'll want the pelt off."

Winna considered this for a moment. "Shave the skin. I want to have the gloves be an extension of my own skin. I'll use resin to help me grip the twelve spears you've made me." She looked down at his hands, which deftly shaved the vole's skin. He then extended the tiny pelt between two sticks in the ground where he would build his fire.

"You'll see this skin will suit your needs. I've already prepared two dozen like it. I'll sew them together tonight. You can drop by for them right here tomorrow morning. By then I should have heard from my friend the crow." As he said this, Wiglaff made the fire spring to life. A curl of smoke rose up through the pines and oaks around the small clearing. Wiglaff and Winna heard the bounding of deer which had smelled the burning wood of the fire. As her brother once again went into a trance, Winna withdrew. She returned to their village to help the warriors prepare for battle.

Mordru was glad to see her. "Do you think you can prevail upon your worthless brother to make a few more spears before tomorrow morning?" He was clearly upset at the prospect of fighting with insufficient weapons.

"Wiglaff is on a mission to discover which villages are for us and which are against. He'll know by tomorrow morning. Do you think the information will be important?"

Mordru contemplated that for a moment. "All right. After Wiglaff reports on the enemy tomorrow morning, he can make more spears. We have precious few to fight the large enemy force assembling against us. As for you, what do you intend to do to help?"

Winna set her jaw and said, "Wiglaff is fashioning vole skin gloves so I can wield my spears. I'll be ready to fight by noon tomorrow. Right now I'd like to distribute pine resin to all your warriors if you'll let me do so."

Mordru nodded. "We've had good luck so far in battle. But luck may not be enough against what we'll face in the next few days. Numbers matter. If only we could reduce the numbers of the enemy while brewing up a diversion and causing fear at the same time." He then turned to hearten his troops with stories and plans for their defense. As he spoke stridently to the rapt audience of men around the fire in the village square, Winna deftly moved among them dispensing resin dust, which they gratefully rubbed between their hands. When she had finished her task, Winna withdrew and sought Wiglaff to tell him of their father's needs.

She discovered her brother sewing together her vole-skin hand coverings. He asked her to hold up her hands so he could fit the skins over them. The skins he had prepared were shriveled and shrunken from having been soaked and dried, but they would stretch and become smooth as he pulled them to fit. He trimmed the sewn skins and adjusted them on her hands, so each of her fingers fit through a different opening. He made two hand coverings exactly the same and stretched them as he worked them down her palms and tied them at her wrists. She worked her fingers when they were tight over her palms, and then she applied powdery resin on both her bare fingers and the skins. Wiglaff handed her a spear so she could wield it. She smiled as she tossed it from hand to hand.

"The skins work perfectly. See how when I hold the spear with both hands, the shaft will not slip?" She hit the butt of the spear on the ground, then placed it against her foot and lowered the pointed end with the flint head toward an imaginary enemy. She did a few more maneuvers, jabbing and slicing in the air. Finally, she extended the spear at full length, the base of the shaft in one hand. She lunged forward, then wheeled around in a wide, slicing motion. "No more blisters!" Winna said with a laugh while she joined Wiglaff for a dinner of nuts, seeds, and fruit. She noticed her brother had fetched another live vole, which cowered in the cage by the fire.

"Oh, our father wants you to fashion more spears. He's worried we won't have enough for the battle. He also wants a diversion and something to frighten the attackers." She hesitated and wondered whether Wiglaff had heard what she said.

After a few moments, he raised his head from looking into the fire. "He'll have his diversion, and the enemy will be afraid. If you look in the armory, you'll find I've added two dozen spears with the flint heads. The others may not have noticed the additions. They don't notice much anyway. Tell Father not to worry about the diversion he wants. As for fright, my crow will help with that."

Winna looked doubtful. Her brother was always being cryptic. "Can you be more specific? Father will understand what he sees ... like the spears. He hates innuendo and visions. You know that. Give me details! Otherwise, I won't tell him anything."

Wiglaff looked toward the setting sun. The forest was already darkening in anticipation of nightfall. He put more wood on his fire before he spoke. "What makes villagers more fearful than anything else?" He asked to answer her question with one of his own.

"They fear the unknown. They fear the uncontrollable. They fear the certainty of death."

Wiglaff nodded. "You remember those fears from when we talked before. Good." He reached behind his back and brought out a small container containing a viscous, black liquid. "I made this just for the occasion. It answers all the fears you named."

Winna said, "All I see is a gummy, black liquid."

"That's all it appears to be. But it's a strong poison. I cooked some special beans and was really careful to avoid the fumes. Do you want a demonstration of the poison's power?" He did not wait for an answer but dipped the end of a twig in the liquid and extended it toward the vole's mouth. The animal licked its lips where the applied liquid lay. Then the vole arched its back, shuddered and expired. Quickly, Wiglaff removed the vole from its cage and cut off its head. He gutted the creature, careful to put aside the contaminated head and innards. He sliced the corpse into sections. "Do you have any questions?" he asked her with a grim smile.

Winna asked, "How will this poison help us in the fight?"

"You will not be joining our father's warriors, will you?" Wiglaff asked while contemplating the pieces of raw vole that lay bloody on the ground before him.

Winna's lips pressed together, and her eyes flashed with disappointment. "You know I'll never be accepted among them. Why do you ask?"

Wiglaff smiled. "More can be done from the outside of the main fighting force than from within it. Let's say you use your bow. You dip your arrowheads in this viscous liquid and shoot the enemy from a hiding place."

Winna smiled too. She reached for the container with the poison, but Wiglaff held out his hand to stop her. "This poison is strong; you'll have to take special precautions. If the smallest drop of poison gets on your fingers or in your mouth or eyes, nothing can save you from its effects. One more thing, if it is poured on a fire, the smoke from that fire will kill anyone who inhales it."

She knit her brow and asked, "Why are you telling me this? Are you trying to scare me?"

Wiglaff looked sad. "I'm trying to save your life. I'm also suggesting that after you wound several of them, you should go to their villages and, one by one, put the poison in their village fires. An arrow having its arrowhead dipped in the poison should be enough. Just don't be downwind when you shoot the arrows into the fire. If the enemy should surround or capture you, use your poisoned arrows to cut yourself free."

She nodded, now fully understanding her mission. Wiglaff handed her the container with the poison. She handled it carefully as she walked it back to the village. Behind her, she heard the sound of a crow cawing and her brother's answering caws, in a now familiar rhythm. Evidently, the messenger crow had returned with the required information. She would return in the morning to obtain the message for their father.

Mordru was still stirring the hearts of his troops with the kind of language warriors like to hear. Seeing Winna approach the fire, he told his second in command to continue inspiring his troops while he spoke with his daughter. They walked out of earshot of the warriors to talk.

"So what does your brother Wiglaff say about the additional spears?" Mordru asked.

Winna nodded and gestured for her father to follow her to the armory hut.

"As you can see, Wiglaff has provided many additional spears."

Mordru examined one spear carefully. Then he counted the spears. "I hate to admit it, but these spears are good quality, and forty are sufficient for our current needs. What else did Wiglaff say?"

"He gave me a poisonous potion that he made especially for me. Father, he plans for me to go ahead of your men and use the poison on my arrows, so at a distance, I can cause the fear you wanted."

Mordru considered what his daughter said. "I'm not easy about having to send you on this dangerous mission, well ahead of my warriors, but I can't deny the wisdom of doing so." With a nod, he blessed the idea.

While Mordru returned to the fire and his men, Winna gathered two bows and two dozen arrows. She applied poison to the arrowheads, careful not to get the gummy substance on her fingers. Winna had plenty of poison left over to use on the enemy fires. After hiding the poisoned arrows, the bows and the container of poison where no one was likely to find them, she stood outside the magical circle of warriors to hear what her father had to tell them. Her heart leapt with anticipation of glorious battle. She remembered her first kill on behalf of her village and thirsted for more enemy blood. Her only regret was that she might not be able to save her father a second time from death if she was out wreaking havoc on the enemy. She resolved to raise this issue with Wiglaff at dawn.

***

Wiglaff was seated before the embers of his fire. The crow had long since flown. Between the boy's thumb and index finger of his right hand were two eagle feathers.

"Brother, are you still in your trance? Can you hear me? It's dawn."

Wiglaff stirred and gazed at his sister. She came into focus. "Hello, Winna. Are the arrows ready? I'm afraid you'll have to leave immediately. The raiders are on the march toward our village. Mother dropped by earlier with more poison in case we need it."

Winna's surprise caused her eyes to widen, "So our mother is a part of this plan?"

"She's the one who suggested the poison. It was her castor bean recipe that gave us the sticky liquid. So we're all involved. I think you should take this new pot of poison with you. Use it as you see fit." Wiglaff handed her a large container of poison looking just like the last batch he gave her.

"Before I go, what about our father's protection? The last time he was threatened, I was there to stop his attacker. This time I'll be far away. Who will help him?" She looked concerned.

Wiglaff said, "The crow told me if you act swiftly, the enemy will never be able to attack our village. The trick will be to hit their leaders with poisoned arrows while they advance. That will make them confused. If their villages are also threatened, they'll put off their attack to the future. We'll have time to prepare an alliance before their next attack."

As she was departing on her mission, Wiglaff called out, "Be careful and return alive. I've done all I can to guarantee our success," as he held up the two eagle feathers. "All the enemy villages are along the riverbank on the sunrise side. The river divides our friends from our foes."

Winna nodded over her shoulder. Nimble-footed, she made her way to the place in the forest where her bows and arrows were hidden. Slinging the quiver over one shoulder and the bows across her chest, she held one poison pot in each hand. She headed across the river and ran along the riverbank toward the advancing attackers.

When she saw the chief of the enemy clan and his men, who were all painted blue, she crouched by a tree and waited with an arrow in her bow. Around the tree, she aimed and let the arrow fly into the thigh of the chief. The man screamed in outrage and fell on the ground writhing in pain. By the time he had landed, Winna was racing through the woods toward the next line of advancing warriors. Again, she shot from behind a large tree and hit the leader in the gut with her poisoned arrow. Moving stealthily forward through the brush and thin tree line toward the third group of clansmen, Winna made sure to balance the two pots of poison. By this time, messengers from the first two villages were running toward the same place as she, shouting that their leaders had been slain.

For the third time, Winna took aim and let her arrow fly into the chest of the last leader of the raiding party. The poison was not needed as the man received the weapon in his heart. The female child-warrior now raced forward along the river to take care of the enemy villages, one by one.

Outside of the first village, Winna screamed like a scared child at the top of her lungs, "Our chief is dead! They've killed our chief! They shot him with an arrow. All is lost!"

There was no fire burning in the village square, so Winna waited until the chief's woman emerged from her hut beating her breasts and tearing at her hair in grief at the news. An arrow took care of her woeful lamentations.

By mid-morning, Winna arrived at the next village. Luckily, there was a fire blazing in the village square, so Winna dipped her already poisoned arrow in the sticky substance to be sure there was enough to do the job. She let her arrow fly into the fire. As women came out of their huts, Winna evaluated which were the elders.

Winna released two arrows in quick succession at the elders she guessed were the leaders. Their dead bodies and the poisonous smoke from the fire caused enough confusion and fear that Winna was able to sneak off and proceed to the third village by noon.

Winna knew that her progress among the communities would form a pattern. The raiders would be able to follow the path of her destruction. She began thinking about what she would do if she were attacked from behind. An idea came to her in a flash. She would cross the river and follow it back down the other side to her own village. By taking that path, she would run among tribes friendly to Mordru. As she was not painted blue and having blue eyes and red hair, she would be recognized as a child of the villages and not be bothered.

With her escape plan decided, she continued to move toward the next village in the alliance against her people. So she despoiled the fourth, fifth and sixth villages going upriver leaving her poison pots in the flames of the last two villages' fires. Winna left villagers moaning and dying in her wake. At the river's edge, she planted all but two of her remaining arrows in an arc around her position. With their notches pressed down and their poisoned arrowheads pointed upward at an angle, pursuing warriors would be impaled. She caught her breath for a moment, glad to take the time to recover while the pain in her side dissipated. Her feet and legs bled from running through the rough country, but she did not care because she had all but completed her mission without mishap.

As evening fell, a group of ten tall warriors in blue paint raced toward her. Unperturbed, she shot the leading men in the chest. Then she dove into the river and swam to the opposite bank. The eight surviving warriors ran straight into her trap where the planted arrows dug into their flesh. From the opposite bank of the river, Winna watched the eight attackers die in agony from the poison on the arrows. Winna, now confident she had slain all her pursuers, began her journey home, loping past village after village, her red hair flying like a flag behind her. When villagers did see her, she waved cheerily, her two bows slung across her chest and her empty quiver bouncing on her back.

By the time Winna got back to her village, it was past midnight, and Winna did not go straight to her parents' hut but sought out Wiglaff who was sitting in his usual place waiting for her. He smiled when she stood before him, her face reddened from exercise and her eyes dancing wild in the firelight with her sense of accomplishment.

"Brother, I did what you said. As you see, I'm back home safe. Have you heard news of our father and his warriors?"

Wiglaff gestured for his sister to sit down for a moment. He smiled and examined bones he had arranged on the ground that now lay between them, on either side of a line he had drawn in the soil.

Winna recognized the pattern immediately. The six neck bones to her left were the six villages she had attacked on the other side of the river. By each Wiglaff had made an X. In the diagram where Winna had attacked the leaders of each enemy village, there was a black crow's feather. Two eagle feathers were stuck in the ground outside the bone symbol for the first village she had attacked.

Wiglaff told her, "You probably have guessed what my drawing means." He used his fingers to point out each feature on the display he had created. "You ran upriver and struck in these eight places. Then, in a moment of insight, you created a trap for the enemy before you swam across the river to safety. You came back downriver on our side all the way without being followed." He looked up and pointed to her empty quiver. "You used all your arrows, and I notice you no longer carry the poison pots. You've still got your two bows and quiver. You've scratched your legs a little, and your feet are bleeding. Otherwise, you're fine. As soon as you've caught your breath, you should tell mother you're all right."

Winna nodded sagely. She had no idea how Wiglaff knew her progress on the other side of the river. A crow cawed in a nearby tree. She said, "The crow must have brought you word of what I did."

The boy nodded and raised a bit of raw meat to reward his messenger bird. The crow flapped down to eat it. "Eat hearty, my crow. You did well."

Simultaneously, a giant eagle landed on the bough the crow had abandoned. It shook its feathers and preened. Wiglaff offered the eagle a larger chunk than he had given the crow. The huge bird dropped to the ground.

Wiglaff handed the remaining meat to Winna. "You feed the eagle. It came unbidden, but it came for you."

She fed the fresh meat to the bird, which flew off immediately after its beak grasped the offering. Winna rose and nodded goodbye.

***

Back in the village, Onna was waiting to hear the news.

"Mother, I'm back," Winna said as she hugged her.

"I knew you'd be all right. Before you come into the hut, put your bows back in the armory and bury your contaminated quiver by the oak tree to the rear of the hut. Do these things quickly before your father and his warriors arrive. I've got some herbal ointment and cloth to fix your scratches before you change your clothes. Don't say anything to anyone about what you've been up to. I know you told Wiglaff, but that's okay."

Winna did as her mother requested. Inside her family's hut, Onna washed and wiped her daughter's bloody legs and feet. She applied the ointment to the cuts briars and brambles had made. She laid aside Winna's blood-soaked deerskin shoes and gave her a new pair that fit better than the last.

Winna was bursting to tell her mother what had happened, but each time she opened her mouth, Onna raised two fingers to her lips. Onna knew the power of silence. She also knew her daughter needed to learn the virtue of secrecy.

"Daughter, many will criticize what happened today. Revenge has long talons. No one knows you were the cause of the enemy's discomfort and defeat. It is better they never know."

Winna was excited about her exploits and wanted recognition. "Shouldn't father know the truth?"

Onna smiled. "Your father is the last person who needs to know the truth. If anyone asks him, he will have no personal knowledge of what was done. He can justly claim he knows no man who shot and poisoned the enemy leadership and wreaked havoc on their villages. It will be assumed that an unnamed scourge laid our enemies low, not a human. Your legend will be the mystery behind our success. The quieter you remain, the greater your role in the victory. Men will swell with pride and brag about their exploits today in battle. Let them believe they are invincible."

"And Wiglaff, what of his role in today's battle?" Winna asked her mother. "Will his role remain a mystery too?"

Onna smiled and asked, "What role are you talking about, Winna? Your brother was sitting in his clearing talking with birds all yesterday and today. He played no role whatsoever. Even if he had done so, who would believe it? His father always said he'd never be a warrior. He'd deny his involvement."

Winna was finally grasping the wisdom of her mother's words, but another thought crossed her mind. She had to ask the question. "Mother, did you concoct the black liquid that caused our victory?"

Onna squinted at her daughter and said, "I don't know what you're talking about."

Winna crossed her arms over her chest and said with deep sarcasm, "Whatever the truth is, I hope you won't stir anything like what I used to coat my arrowheads in our dinner stew."

Onna now smiled. "I'd never mix incompatible sauces any more than your brother would feed to a crow the same feast as he gives an eagle."

Winna smiled too. She did not contradict her mother or volunteer the information that she, not her brother, had fed the eagle. The mother and daughter shared dried venison, seeds with honey and dried fruit. Onna then urged her daughter to sleep for a while before her father's return from battle. So Winna crawled under her bear's skin and collapsed, exhausted after her exciting day. Onna hummed while her daughter slept.

The next morning, Mordru and all his warriors returned to the village. Some had been wounded in battle. Mordru ordered a bonfire built in the village square and set three aged deer near the fire to roast. He also placed swords in the fire in preparation for cauterizing wounds. While the warriors boasted of their exploits and ate venison, the screams of the men whose wounds were closed by red hot blades, broke the revelry and underscored the fact that risks had been taken that might have cost lives and limbs. One valiant warrior who had been sliced in the arm and leg bellowed until Mordru made the man bite on a strip of leather to keep him from swallowing his tongue and to distract him from his pain. He joked the man should consider such wounds superficial, and he bared his arm and waist to show what he meant.

One reason Mordru drew universal respect were the horrid wounds whose vicious scars covered his body. He liked to tell the story of each wound and thereby serve as an example of valor to his warriors. He had named his scars from his head to his waist before Winna appeared in her new skins and shoes. Her hair was tied back with a thong of deerskin. All warriors' eyes were fixed on her graceful movements in the firelight.

To bring his troops' attention back to the battle, Mordru called out the question, "Where is my worthless son Wiglaff, who missed yesterday's battles altogether?"

Winna said, "Father, he's in his clearing casting bones and talking with birds. He's been there the last two days. Would you like me to fetch him here?"

Mordru sneered at the idea and shook his head. Another warrior screamed in agony as the hot blade touched his wound. "Tell my strange son he'll never know the pleasure or the pain of being a warrior, any more than our women will. What say you to that, daughter?"

Winna's eyes darted fire, but she held her peace. "We women like our men brave, and our brave men like our women pliable."

"Aye, and willing," said one warrior.

"Aye, and able," echoed another. "How old are you now Winna?" he continued, pressing his luck.

Mordru, sensing danger in the direction of the banter, said, "Any who wants to address Winna should consider whether he'd first like to taste my blade." He held up the red-hot iron, and then he laid it on another gaping wound. The scream that resulted made his point. The huge leader thrust the blade back in the fire. His dagger cut off a hunk of venison, which he ate with relish. His eyes went from one warrior to another daring him to speak.

Satisfied that he had everyone's attention again, he said, "Where was I? Ah yes, I had reached my waist, and now if my daughter will return to our hut, I'll count the scars from my waist to my toes." Mordru waited until Winna was gone before he disrobed completely to finish his stories.

It was well past nightfall when the warriors went to their huts to join their families. That included the hero Mordru. Onna was awake to receive him in her arms. Winna heard them through the night. Not a word was spoken by either of anything Wiglaff or Winna had done. Onna was too wise to contradict her husband as he ranged from boasts to endearments. She always said her husband was never wrong. They never argued. They were the most loving pair Winna ever knew.

The next morning the enemy raiders came to make peace. Onna urged Mordru to hear them and judge their proposed terms for himself. A truce was called whereby warriors on both sides of the river promised not to cross the river with arms. Mordru agreed to their terms. When the leader of the enemy alliance asked how Mordru had managed to kill all their best warriors at the same time as most of their leading women who were still in the villages, Mordru answered he knew nothing about the mysteries of war, only the taste of weapons. Not satisfied with this answer, the enemy went back to their side of the river sullen but resigned to keep their truce. They were afraid what might happen if they broke the peace. Still, they knew the day would come when they would fight again to be avenged for their losses.

When Mordru told Onna the terms of the truce, she nodded and said, "Husband, you've done well. Those blue skins will regroup and fight again, but not for a long while. In this time of peace, we'll prepare for war and watch for signs of aggression."

Winna learned the terms of the truce from Onna. She relayed them to Wiglaff and asked him what he thought.

"Sister, war is a condition of existence. You and I have this year come of age. You have tasted blood and bled too. I have watched you grow. You are a marvel, and you've just begun as a warrior. Has any of our father's men appealed to you as a possible mate?"

She blushed and shook her head. "None compares with our father. I could marry no lesser man than what he is."

Wiglaff stirred the ground with his stick and looked out over the treetops to watch birds flying just under the clouds. She noticed his jet-black eyes had a sad, faraway look. His dark brown hair was tangled and matted, and he wore a strip of leather around his head.

"What are you thinking, brother? Your eyes look so sad."

"I was just thinking about the future … endless war, endless begetting, fleeting happiness. What is life, Winna?"

Winna knew her brother's moods. "Your thoughts travel too dark for me by far, Wiglaff. Have you been gazing into the future again? Will you tell me what you saw?"

He smiled ruefully. "I just told you, but you weren't listening. It's all right. Right now I've got to get back to my divination. My birds are coming soon for their instructions. Don't mind me. Drop back anytime. Goodbye for now."

Winna knew she had been dismissed. She wanted to say more. She wanted her brother to communicate with her. This was not the time. As she walked back toward the village, she heard the beating of great wings. Two vultures swooped down to eat what Wiglaff fed them. Hearing small bird sounds, she could not determine whether they came from the vultures or from her brother.

***

Onna and Winna had long conversations while Mordru trained his warriors for their next battles. "The old warrior teaches that the next war is always different from the last. He pushes his men to the limit of their endurance. They never complain because they know the cost is their leader's displeasure. A single frown from Mordru lasts for months. Each would die for him, and many will."

"Yet I, a female warrior, am outside the magic circle of the men," Winna lamented.

Onna nodded and said, "You have a greater purpose than to die like a man. Your brother has seen a vision of your future. He says you'll save all our villages through nurturing warrior women like yourself."

Winna looked down to break the fixed eyes of her mother. "He never mentioned that to me. Did he say that before or after what I did across the river?"

Her mother looked down at the hides she was sewing together. "It was just after ... before you came back to visit him. Does it really matter, though, when he had the vision?"

Winna said, "I suppose not. Please pass that patch of deerskin. It will just fit the empty place in Wiglaff's new coat I'm making for him."

Onna's red hair was streaked with gray. Her ice blue eyes seemed cold to some, but to Winna, they were wise and loving. "What are you thinking, daughter? I know you're troubled by something. Will you tell me now or do you want to wait to let things settle?"

"It's just I've been thinking of what Wiglaff said at our last meeting. He was talking as if he was in one of his trances. It frightened me to have him speak of the things in life as if they had already happened as if he had seen them all already. He was so sad and lonely." This made Winna melancholy, she paused to let her mother dwell on what she had said. "He asked me whether I had found a warrior who could be my mate."

Onna's eyes went wide. "Well, have you?"

Winna answered, "Of course not. I told my brother I could only marry a man equal to or better than our father, whose like I've never seen. In fact, I may never see such a man."

Onna reflected on this for a while. "Warriors are not the only possible mates for such as you and me." She did not elaborate. "It's early, though, to think of marriage for two people just coming into manhood and womanhood. What do you think about forming a group of young women warriors like yourself?"

"As in the vision Wiglaff had for me? I'll have to talk with him about that. I've never found the like of me among girls or boys, or women or men for that matter." She stitched together the last piece of Wiglaff's new coat. She stood and dusted the deerskin coat off. Trying it on, she modeled it for her mother.

"Well done, Winna. He's bound to like it. Are you going to take it to him this afternoon?"

Winna smiled, hugging the coat around her shoulders. She and her brother were the same height, so whatever fit her would surely fit him. "Yes, I'll do that. Then I'll come back and help with preparing dinner. Do you have anything for me to take to him? Food? Messages?"

Onna thought for a moment. "Ask him whether he thinks he's ready to study with a master of what he's already good at."

"A master? What kind of master, mother?" Winna had stopped parading the deerskin coat. She searched her mother's eyes as if to discover the meaning of what she had just said.

"I mean a shaman. I know the most adept shaman of our time. I can make the introduction, but Wiglaff must make the decision. I've mentioned the possibility a few times, but he's always maintained he's not yet ready. After what's happened recently, I think he's more than ready."

"The thought gives me the shivers, Mother." She noticed her mother flinched when she used the word 'shivers.' She instinctively changed her perspective and approached the subject from a new direction. "What makes you think Wiglaff's ready now to become the apprentice of a shaman?"

Onna nodded her understanding of her daughter's question. "As I've taught you since birth, there are two types of men. One is the warrior. Your father is the finest of the warrior breed. To be a great warrior, you have to be born one."

"You said two types of men. What's the other kind?"

"The other kind is the shaman, of which very few exist. Those are the visionaries … the seerers. They also have to be born. There is no way to train for this unless you have all the gifts from birth. Your brother has all those gifts. When he first came, he got a look that scared me it was so earnest and deep and serious. He never wanted to smile because it broke a connection between him and his visions. He not only understood what animals and men were thinking, but he also could communicate with both on a level I would not have thought possible if I hadn't witnessed it first hand. I recognized his gifts because I once knew a man who exemplified the ways of the shaman in the same way as your father exemplifies the warrior."

"And you chose the warrior."

"Because the warrior chose me," Onna said cryptically.

"And the shaman did not?" Winna pursued without realizing the pain she was causing by doing so.

Onna wept quietly and shook her head. "Once troth has been plighted, the seal is done. You live with your choice. If that did not hold, the world would come unhinged, at least for me. You'd better hurry to deliver the new coat to Wiglaff. You won't be back to help with dinner if you don't go right now." Onna wiped her eyes.

Winna felt uncomfortable about pursuing the matter further. She turned and walked through the door into the afternoon sunlight streaming through the forest. Rushing to the opening where her brother dwelled, Winna mulled over her mother's distinction between the warrior and the shaman. She mused, *Could it be that my mother loved a shaman once? Did Mother regret choosing Mordru as her mate? Why is she weeping?*

Wiglaff was looking at a plant with aphids strung along its stem. Ants were running from aphid to aphid milking a liquid from each. "Winna, you've come just in time to see the ants milking the aphids. See how the aphids are eating the stem of the plant?" She nodded. "See how each aphid has its own ant pressing its body to get a bubble of moisture?" She nodded again. "People are like aphids and ants, I think," Wiglaff said.

Winna did not want to follow her brother's strange logic. Instead, she took off the deerskin coat she was wearing and handed it to him. "I made you this coat. Please try it on."

Wiglaff took off his tattered clothing and stuck his arms into the sleeves of the new coat. It fit him perfectly. He smiled shyly. "It's nice and warm. The leather is smooth. Thank you."

She hugged him. Standing back, she gestured for him to turn around, nodding when he had made a circle and faced her again. "So what do you think?" Winna asked.

"It's beautiful. You're more than a perfect warrior, you're the perfect tailor too. I'll be warm this winter, thanks to you. Maybe I can repay you by making you a fur hat. Would you like that?"

She beamed. "I'd love it. Oh, thank you. You don't have to repay me if you don't want to."

Wiglaff said, "But I do want to. Would you like a beaver hat?"

"Beaver would be nice. It would go with the color of my hair."

He nodded, looking at his sister while visualizing what she would look like in the hat.

"Wiglaff, Mother asked whether you are ready to start training with her friend the shaman."

He seemed startled by her sudden shift in subject. He became serious and said, "Tell Mother I'm now ready to become the apprentice to the shaman she knows. I learned I was ready only in the last few days. Her question comes at the perfect time."

"When I left her, Mother was weeping. Maybe you can tell me why." She explained the conversation she just had with Onna about the two types of men, the warrior, and the shaman. "Why would she have wept when she talked about the shaman? Do you know?"

Wiglaff got a faraway look in his eyes, and Winna for a moment thought she was going to lose him as he drifted into one of his trances. Instead, he said, "Long ago when she was a maid, Mother had many suitors, but only two mattered to her, a warrior and a shaman. She was conflicted because she could not marry both of her suitors, so she waited. Our father asked her to marry him before his rival did. That's why Mordru is our father. It's also why you are a female warrior."

"But it doesn't explain why you're becoming the apprentice to a shaman." Winna's eyes probed her brother's for the answer."

Wiglaff laughed silently and said, "I'm strange."

"You're what?"

"You heard me. I'm strange. Admit it. I've always been a great disappointment to our father. The supreme warrior's eldest son, I'm definitely not a warrior. Everyone knows that, even you. I'm the other thing entirely. I'm not only the opposite of him, but I'm the opposite of you. Somehow I'm an expression of something in our mother that our father chooses to ignore."

Winna, who liked clarity, was confused by Wiglaff's analysis. "Are you saying you think you're not our father's son? Why that would mean that Onna conceived you with another man."

"Wait, Winna, I'm not saying what you suggest at all. I'm definitely Mordru's son, though he is loath to admit the fact. On a number of occasions, I honestly thought he wished me dead. He plunged me into an icy stream at birth. He cut a hole in the frozen river and dunked me in, naked and screaming, on my birthday each year afterward until I was five years old. The trouble was, each time he tried to rid himself of me, I became more of what he hated. My powers grew the more he hated them. I feared him and challenged him too. I became the person he loved to hate. In a way, we defined each other. Fortunately, for you, this worked to your advantage. You became the warrior son he always wished I'd be."

Winna thought about this for a few minutes. Then she said, "Mother said I should ask you about your vision for the women warriors. You never mentioned your vision to me. What was it? How do I fit in?"

Wiglaff did not hesitate since his vision had been clear. "I pictured you with women you selected from all the friendly villages. You trained them to be warriors better than all the men. You and they won every battle, not by being brash and forthright, but by being stealthy and smart. In the future, our village's challenges will be dwarfed by larger foes than we've ever known. Only by your brave, lonely efforts will we manage to survive."

"So you think I should start right away to form this group of women warriors?"

"I can't demand it, but I'm sure of what I saw. You will do this, and your actions will assure our people's survival. It's up to you what you do. I know you'll choose wisely. Your recent exploits indicate what you can do alone. Just think what might happen if there were … say, twenty of you!"

Winna thought for a moment. Then she brightened up. "I just remembered I've got to help Mother fix dinner. Are you coming?"

Wiglaff said, "Later, perhaps, I'll come. I have a few things to tidy up here first." He seemed to become distracted and puttered around, lifting his divination bones and placing them in a pouch with a drawstring. A crow flew down and perched on his shoulder. Absentmindedly, he rubbed its beak with his forefinger.

Winna shook her head as she watched her brother retreat into his shell. Then using her martial stride, she walked rapidly back to the village to help her mother fix dinner.

CHAPTER TWO

The Wild Child

"A feral child (also called wild child) is a human child who has lived isolated from human contact from a very young age where they have little or no experience of human care, behavior, or, crucially, of human language. Some feral children have been confined by people (usually their own parents), and in some cases this child abandonment was due to the parents' rejection of a child's severe intellectual or physical impairment. Feral children may have experienced severe abuse or trauma before being abandoned or running away. Feral children are sometimes the subjects of folklore and legends, typically portrayed as having been raised by animals."
—https://en.wikipedia.org/wiki/Feral_child

SEVERAL months later, Wiglaff found what at first he thought was a wild child hiding in the gorse by the riverbank. She blended so well with the background that he would have missed her altogether if she hadn't sneezed. Her hair was tangled with twigs and flowers twisted here and there. She was dressed in a hodgepodge of skins barely stitched together. She whimpered when he parted the foliage to see the creature that had made the sneezing sound. She was almost as emaciated as he. Covered as she was with dried mud and blue paint, her hunger made her eyes seem large and entreating. Wiglaff nodded at her and turned to allow her privacy. After taking a few steps, he looked back to find she had emerged from cover to follow him.

The early morning was the best time to hunt new mushrooms. Wiglaff had gathered several. He offered one to the girl. Examining his gift carefully before she took it, she held it in her hand and hesitated. He made a show of eating a mushroom exactly like it. Reassured, she smiled and ate hers greedily. Continuing his hunt, he occasionally stooped to pick other mushrooms. The girl imitated his actions, but she clearly did not know how to recognize edible spores. Wiglaff stopped her from eating a poisonous toadstool, and taking it from her he flung it into the woods. Then he handed her another good mushroom. After she had eaten it, he realized she must still be hungry. Giving her a strip of dried venison, she chewed while watching him harvest.

Both Wiglaff and the girl walked quietly scanning the ground as they went. Forest creatures were not frightened by their approach. The girl tugged at his deer hide jacket and pointed to a sow and her brood rooting for acorns and truffles under a wide oak tree.

"The boar will be nearby." Those were her first words to him. He put his finger to his lips and gestured for her to follow. He made a cawing sound that lured a crow which landed on his shoulder. Wiglaff stroked the bird's beak and talked crow language until the bird flew in circles, stopping on boughs occasionally. It then returned to Wiglaff's shoulder and cawed emphatically.

Wiglaff whispered, "Don't worry about the boar. It was killed by hunters not far from here. The sow will take care of her brood." She nodded, apparently unimpressed that Wiglaff had learned this from the crow.

"My name is Freia. What's yours?" She did not look at him when she asked his name. While she waited for his answer, she seemed preoccupied with scanning the forest. The answer was a long time coming, but she was patient.

"My name is Wiglaff. I live in the village that lies in the direction of the rising sun over there." He pointed toward the village. "Where do you live?"

She shook her head. Then she spread her arms wide. "I live in the forest." She shook her head and chewed on her strip of deer jerky. "My village was destroyed. I am alone." She smiled ruefully.

Wiglaff said, "My village was not destroyed, yet I like to be alone. I like to let the forest talk to me."

She cocked her head at him and asked, "Do you want me to leave you alone?"

Wiglaff thought about that for a moment. With a faraway look, he said, "Suit yourself." He paused. Then he looked at her sternly and continued, "Just don't interrupt me when I grow silent and enter my private world."

She smiled. "While she lived, my mother had a secret world." Now the girl was the one with the faraway look in her eyes. Changing mood, she brightened and said, "I have a magic stone. Do you want to see it?" Not waiting for an answer, she revealed a small pouch with a drawstring. From it, she extracted a clear crystal stone, which glistened in the sunlight.

Wiglaff nodded but kept walking. She shrugged and put her stone away.

Over his shoulder he asked her, "Do you want shelter in my village? You'd be welcome in my family's hut. My brothers and sisters would be good company. There's always plenty to eat."

She walked for a time while she brooded on his invitation. "Do you stay in your family's hut?"

Wiglaff said, "No. It's noisy and bustling. I like to stay in my forest clearing. It's quiet there." His eyes searched in the direction of his make-shift home.

She caught up with him. "I'll stay there too. Say, isn't this a beautiful day?" She smiled at the sunlight streaming through the trees and falling on the ferns and mosses. Motes rose and fell in a constant dance through the shafts of light.

Wiglaff looked where she was gazing. He saw insects swarming in a cloud. "Wait here for a minute." He walked into the woods and found a clearing where a horde of flies was buzzing around bloody remains. The girl came up beside him and put her hand over her mouth.

Seeing her horror, Wiglaff remarked, "You couldn't wait, could you?"

"What happened here?" she exclaimed.

"I think this is where the hunters slew the boar. They cut off the animal's head and gutted it." He pointed to the bloody head and the animal's line of entrails. Continuing to use his fingers as pointers, he cataloged what he saw. "There are its heart and liver. The brains are still in the skull. Whoever did this is wasteful." As he approached the remains, Wiglaff waved his hands to keep the flies away. The girl followed close behind him waving her hands. Flies were everywhere.

He stopped. "Here, take the mushrooms," he ordered her. She took them and watched while he harvested the boar's heart, liver, and brains. Blood dripped through his fingers while he searched for tough vine which was long enough to bind the organs together as a parcel. Ivy was perfect for the purpose. While he wrapped the leafy vine and tied it firmly, crows came to dine on what was left. Flies did not bother the carrion birds, and they continued feasting while the crows picked through the entrails.

"What are you going to do?" Freia asked him.

"I'm going to take these boar parts to my mother. She'll be delighted. If you want to come along, you can meet her."

She stepped back, reluctant. "You have dark hair and black eyes, but you don't use blue body paint. What will your mother think of me?" She seemed to be frightened since her people were enemies of Wiglaff's people from across the river. Recent fighting had cost many lives. The truce was tenuous. Another deadly skirmish could erupt at the least provocation. Wiglaff ignored her fear and returned a practical observation.

"For one thing," he said with a smile, "she'll see you need to jump in the river to wash. For another thing, she'll want to untangle your hair and comb it. She'll also want to re-stitch your clothing. She'll do the things all mothers do." Wiglaff was serious about this. Freia envisioned what would probably happen.

"Instead of taking me to your family's hut, will you leave me in the clearing where you stay alone? I'll wait for you there."

Wiglaff said, "I'll do that. It's not far. Let's hurry, though. I had not planned on this side trip. I have things to do."

"What kind of things?" she asked, curious.

"Do you always have a thousand questions?" he rejoined. "You'll see if you stick around. Just mind that you don't get in my way."

Wiglaff walked with long strides while Freia scurried to keep up with him. After a while, she stopped and held her side, breathing rapidly. The exertion had hurt her. "Wiglaff, can we rest for a moment?"

He realized she needed rest. "Yes. My sister doesn't tire while walking, but she stays well fed. Breathe deeply." She did so. "That's right. It always works for me."

When she had caught her breath, she asked, "What's your sister's name?"

"Her name's Winna. You're bound to meet her if you stay in my clearing. She drops by once a day to spy on me for my mother."

"Well, I won't tattle on you, ever." She looked at her feet while she said this and fumbled to balance the mushrooms she was carrying.

Wiglaff smiled. "You don't have anyone to tattle to anymore, do you?"

She shook her head from side to side. "No, I guess not." A tear ran down her cheek.

He rubbed her tear away with his thumb. "Why cry? Tears do no good."

"Why do anything?" she responded, struggling not to weep. She could not restrain herself. She sobbed uncontrollably with her shoulders trembling and her eyes blinking. He was moved by her anguish. He let her cry without speaking.

When she finished, he started walking again. He gestured with his free arm, and she followed him. He walked at a slower pace this time so she could keep up without becoming exhausted.

By noon, they reached his clearing. He gave her a handful of seeds and dried berries to eat and let her lie on his bearskin. Having eaten greedily, she fell asleep immediately. Wiglaff left to take the boar parts to his mother's hut.

***

"I found boar parts in the forest," he told his mother holding up his ivy-bound parcel. "Heart, liver, and brains! Hunters killed the beast recently but left these parts behind. Oh, yes, I also found a blue-painted girl in the forest. She claimed her entire village was slaughtered. She was alone hiding in some gorse by the river. Her name's Freia. She followed me back to my clearing. She's sleeping there now."

Onna raised her eyebrows. "Why don't you bring the girl here? She can be our guest."

Wiglaff said, "I made the offer, but she wanted to stay where I'm staying. She may change her mind. We'll see. Anyway, I'll be getting back."

Onna was unwrapping the boar parts, pleased to have the windfall. "Thank you for bringing the organs. We'll roast them for dinner. Tell Freia she's welcome. By the way, Winna said she'd be stopping by your clearing on her way back from recruiting. She said she'd be there around nightfall. So she'll have the chance to meet Freia."

Wiglaff thought about this. Then he said, "She will if Freia is still there. I don't know what the child intends to do."

Onna nodded. "Having found you, I suspect she'll be staying as long as you let her."

Wiglaff thought about that for a minute. Then he shook his head. "You don't suppose Freia's village was one of those Winna destroyed in our skirmish with the alliance across the river?"

"You said the girl's painted blue, didn't you?" Onna asked by way of answering him. All villagers just across the river wore the blue paint on their bodies as a marker.

Wiglaff nodded. Then he left the hut and walked back to his clearing, mulling over his mother's idea. *What if Freia lost her family because of Winna? Does that imply an obligation on my family's part or my part to protect the girl? On the other hand, could the girl be a spy?*

Sleeping on his bear pelt, Freia did not look at all sinister. She trembled slightly as if she had a chill. Wiglaff covered her with hides to keep her warm, and he let her nap. Having deposited the mushrooms Freia had carried into a rush basket, he finally got down to doing what he had planned for the day.

From his earliest years, Wiglaff had liked grouping similar things by their properties. An exercise Onna later used with all her children, his mother gave him a pile of acorns to sort. He immediately made three piles, one for whole brown acorns, a second for whole green ones and a third for broken acorns and acorn caps. From there he went to grouping forest leaves, making piles of similar ones and noting the trees from which they had fallen.

River stones he particularly liked to sort by color, size, and quality. In this way, he determined which stones were common and which unusual. Wiglaff collected a vast number of odd rocks and favored clear and translucent ones, except for his favorite, the opaque dun red stone that felt smooth and warm in his palm.

Categorization of physical items was the beginning of his categorizing many other things, sounds, and even ideas. By categorization, he associated like with like. Then within these categories, he detected differences. So carrion birds sounded similar, but crows and vultures had distinct cries. Birds sang very different songs in and out of mating season. Their songs also varied by time of day.

Wiglaff learned to imitate the speech of birds, including falcons, hawks, and eagles. When he wandered down the river to the shores of the vast sea, he discovered puffins and seagulls. He also found sea shells and odd wood formations, which he harvested and added to his collections in his clearing.

Today he had planned to make a new set of arrow shafts out of hardwood he had cut to a certain size and shape. He sat on the ground with the rough wooden shafts to his left and the finished shafts to his right. Wiglaff's hands worked rapidly to whittle the shafts with a flint knife. After he had shaped each round shaft, he cut a nock at the base and a seat for the flint arrowhead on the other end. By late afternoon, he had formed forty new shafts.

He had earlier constructed forty flint arrowheads, which he stored in a deerskin pouch tied at the mouth with a drawstring. With a flint knife, he also had cut narrow strips of deer hide. He soaked the pieces in water and pulled them before laying them in a line before him. One by one, he affixed the arrowheads to the arrows and wrapped their bases with the wet deer hide strips, careful to tuck the last twist inside the one before. Once done, he had made forty arrows with nocks and arrowheads. As the wet strips dried and shrunk, the arrowheads would be solidly fixed in place. Then Wiglaff would place them in eight sewn deer-hide quivers, five arrows to each.

Freia awakened just as Wiglaff was moving to his next self-appointed task of fashioning spears. He had placed on the ground ten lengths of hardwood, each the length of a tall warrior. For these he had fashioned large spearheads of flint, sharp around the edges except where they would be fastened to the spears.

"Wiglaff, these arrows are beautifully made." She held and admired one arrow, her eye gauging how straight the shaft seemed.

"Be careful not to cut your fingers. Those flint heads are extremely sharp."

Freia smiled. "I was trained to use a bow and arrow. I can also use spears and knives as my father and brothers once did."

"Let's see how good you are," said Winna, who had crept up silently behind her.

Freia wheeled around to find a red-haired, blue-eyed young woman warrior with a bow slung over her chest, a quiver of arrows at her back and a spear in her hand. The warrior took off her bow and handed it to the stranger and said, "Hit the knot on that pine tree!" Winna pointed at a tree twenty arm-lengths distant. Without hesitation, Freia notched the arrow, aimed and let the arrow fly. It hit the center of the target.

Winna nodded approvingly. She took back her bow and hung it over her chest. Then she handed Freia her spear. "Hurl this spear at the same target." She extended her spear, and the girl grasped it by the shaft.

Freia handled the spear like the expert she was. She balanced the shaft on one finger to find its center of gravity. She eyed the shaft as she twisted it slowly. Finally, she hefted the spear and balanced it in her right hand. She did not throw like a girl with no experience. Instead, she stood like a male warrior and drew back her arm. Her body was graceful as she moved forward and threw the weapon. It struck the intended target right next to the arrow she had already shot.

"Off by a thumb," Winna remarked critically.

"If I hadn't been off by a thumb, I would've ruined a fine arrow. Do you want me to throw again?"

Wiglaff whistled and looked at his sister with his eyebrows raised.

"Brother, can you think of any reason I shouldn't slit this girl's throat right now? Look at her. She's painted blue. She fights like a man. I think she's a threat to us all."

Freia was repositioning herself for a personal attack by Winna. Her eyes flashed defiance. Winna squinted and changed her posture to strike. Wiglaff, however, raised his hand to calm his sister.

"Winna, this is Freia. Freia, this is my sister Winna. I'd like you to hug each other but not with a weapon. Please do so."

The young women warily hugged each other. After they parted, they sized each other up as adversaries will. Winna asked, "Which village across the river is yours?"

"I have no village anymore. My family's village was destroyed. Of my family, I alone survived the poisoned smoke and the battle that followed."

Wiglaff interjected, "I found her in the gorse on our side of the river. She followed me here." He wanted his sister to know the score before she acted impetuously.

Winna's eyes narrowed as she asked, "Freia, how did you, a girl, learn to use weapons like a man?"

Freia bristled and replied, "The same way any self-respecting girl does … by teaching myself. You're clearly a girl warrior. How did you learn to be what you are?"

Winna shrugged. "I decided to be a warrior. Once the decision was made, I then did whatever I could to be the best of the breed. I watched the men train. Since my brother Wiglaff was the best maker of weapons, I learned from him how to judge the worth of arrows, spears, and knives. What he did not teach me, I taught myself."

Wiglaff saw that Freia was impressed. Her eyes widened as she looked from sister to brother and back again. Then she had an afterthought, and her eyes narrowed in suspicion. "Perhaps I've found the reason why my people lost the latest skirmish. I overheard two of our warriors talk about a red-haired, blue-eyed warrior maiden. They said she was fleet of foot and shot arrows at great distances like a goddess. Was that you?"

Wiglaff tried to restrain his sister by raising his hand to silence her, but Winna boldly stated, "I shot well, but not perfectly. All those hit by my arrows died eventually." Wiglaff was appalled by his sister's breach of security, and by his expression, Freia knew Winna spoke the truth.

Freia said, "True, but they died not only because your shafts struck home. You must have used poison."

Wiglaff held his breath and waited. Winna's prowess with a bow was one secret. The poison was an even deeper secret. Freia's guess could jeopardize everything.

For a long while, Winna appraised her rival. She would not answer the question, but her silence was a kind of answer. Freia nodded twice, indicating she knew. She took a step toward Winna, her fingers forming like claws.

Wiglaff intervened by stating, "I fear we've arrived at an impasse, Freia. Soon it will be time for you to choose your destiny. My sister wants to kill you now. Her point of view has merit ... if you die, you'll not be able to inform your people about us." He paused to let the idea sink in. Then he continued, "I think, though, she appreciates the mettle of a girl like herself, another female warrior. Am I right, Winna?"

Winna nodded, waiting for her brother to complete his idea before she made a decision.

Looking directly into Winna's eyes, he asked, "If Freia should decide to become one of your warriors, what would be wrong with that?"

Freia's eyes widened. She never guessed there might be more than one maiden warrior. "Her warriors? Who are they?"

Winna's pride overcame her desire for secrecy. "They are a force that can win in any battle. I command them absolutely. We are invisible because no self-respecting male warrior can admit that we exist."

Freia was intrigued. "Will you tell me more?" She leaned forward with her head cocked to one side. The thought of many women warriors appealed to her imagination.

Winna laughed. "I'll tell you much more … but I have conditions." She arched her brow and watched Freia while she drew her flint knife and ran her fingers along its sharp edges.

Wiglaff now knew his sister and Freia would bargain, so he sighed and went back to his work on the spears while the women deliberated. He was capable of focusing on his handiwork no matter what was happening around him. As the women moved and talked, he matched shafts to spearheads and wrapped them together with wet strips of deer hide as he had done with the arrowheads earlier.

"Conditions?" asked the blue girl, following Winna to retrieve the spear and arrow that were lodged in the pine tree.

Winna, rocking and pulling out her spear, said, "First, we'll go to the river for a long swim. You can swim can't you?"

Freia watched Winna use her knife to dislodge the arrow from the pine. Then she answered, "I swam to get from my side of the river to yours. I can swim the river the long way to the sea or all the way into the mountains to its source. I've done both recently."

"Since it's getting late, let's just swim together. Later we'll make plans for longer swims. Wiglaff, we'll be back before nightfall." Her brother was lost in his work and did not hear her statement. Winna shook her head. She gestured for Freia to follow, and they left the clearing and headed in the direction of the river.

It was dark when Winna and Freia returned from their swim. They were laughing and joking like old friends. Freia no longer wore her mud and blue paint. Her hair was no longer tangled. It did not feature twigs and flowers anymore.

Wiglaff could see her fine muscle tone in the firelight. She no longer looked like a young girl. Instead, she looked like Winna's peer. Her brown eyes, formerly vulnerable and sensitive, were now flashing with the same martial fire that made Winna's eyes piercing and bold.

Winna was telling her exploits in the recent fighting. "So I alone ran from village to village while our men were marching to meet yours, with my arrows I caused as much trouble as possible until I swam the river and returned on this side to my village."

Freia, no longer seeming to be a feral child, hung on Winna's every word. She wanted to be sure of what she had heard. She asked, "You killed everyone in my village single-handedly?"

Winna shook her head. "Not exactly. I might have, but my mission was only to cause fear and confusion so when our clansmen arrived, they could complete the job."

Overhearing this exchange, Wiglaff interjected, "I'm glad to know you've become friends. Sharing such secrets would otherwise be entirely inappropriate."

Winna said, "Freia and I have an agreement. She'll become one of my warriors. She'll also recruit other young women from the villages on the other side of the river."

"What's the wisdom in this, sister?" he asked, genuinely concerned about Winna's idea.

Winna stopped walking and looked her brother in the eyes. "Everyone fights against everyone else all the time. You yourself said that one day, we'll all be confronting forces that dwarf us. Then we'll all need to fight together against the invaders. A way for us to become strong without arousing meddlesomeness and jealousy is through becoming warriors. We can work and train together while all the petty fighting continues, even among the men of our villages."

No longer seeming like a feral child, Freia asserted with her brow knit, "Winna's right. She knows she can't recruit on the other side of the river for many reasons, not least of which is her having personally killed our people in the last skirmishes. I have credibility over there because I'm the lone survivor of my family."

Wiglaff nodded and asked, "What's to stop you from cooperating only until you've learned our secrets? How do we know you can be trusted?"

Freia answered, "You'll have to take the risk. Don't forget, I'm also taking a risk because if my people discover I'm in league with you, they're liable to kill me, but only after cruel torture and interrogation. They'd probably roast me alive. That's the penalty for treachery."

Wiglaff wondered at Freia's transformation from the feral child he had encountered in the woods and this articulate, intelligent and savvy warrior. He seemed satisfied with her answer. He said, "That reminds me. My mother Onna was going to roast the boar organs and brains we found in the forest this morning."

Winna licked her lips hungrily. "Boar? Why didn't you mention it earlier? Come with me, Freia! I'll introduce you to the respectable members of our family over the feast."

Wiglaff watched the two walk in the direction of the village until darkness swallowed them. He gazed into the flames of his fire and became lost in thought.

In the fire, Wiglaff glimpsed the great opponent that would come to subjugate their land. He sensed egregious cruelty. It was a merciless force that might drive all Caledonians to the northern sea if something wasn't done to prevent the catastrophe. Night sounds—insects and frogs— filled the silence. Twigs snapped in the fire. At the fires center, a black and gold salamander crawled out of the log, and

Wiglaff fished it out of the flames on a stick that caught fire in the attempt. The more Wiglaff contemplated the deal Winna had struck with Freia, the greater his appreciation grew for his sister's martial wisdom.

He thought to himself, *What's the worst that could happen? Freia could kill Winna to avenge the loss of her people. The next worse thing would be Winna killing Freia, who now represents the hope of unifying villages on both sides of the river.* As he thought through the situation, he came to another conclusion, *The worst of all outcomes would be the victory of the coming invaders.*

Late that evening, Freia returned alone. She smiled as she told him about her experience. "I met your family. I'm impressed. Your father is a worthy adversary. He's a lot like my fallen father, actually. Your mother is wise and devoted to her home, husband, and children. Of course, Winna's unique. I'm going to enjoy working closely with her. I like your siblings too, the three girls and two boys, yet I can't see how you and Winna can be related to them or to each other. Your siblings seem so … ordinary, by comparison. You and she are like the sun and the moon. Anyway, I'll be staying the night with you here. Tomorrow, Winna's coming for me. Then we'll be planning and training for the future."

Wiglaff nodded. He said, "Sleep on the bear pelt and use the leather covers to keep warm. I won't disturb your slumber. I may be here to say goodbye tomorrow before you leave with Winna. If I'm away, know you can drop by anytime to see me. I'm glad we met by the river this morning. You're the perfect complement to my sister's grand plan."

Freia looked at Wiglaff in the firelight. His angular features were rugged and handsome. "Well, here we are alone by the firelight. Aren't you going to take advantage of me?" When he smiled and shook his head, she said, "I wonder whether I should feel insulted that you won't."

He then looked at her with a gaze she would never forget. She felt it pierce her to the soul. Taking a deep breath, she shrugged and walked over to the bear pelt. She lay there watching the fire and the handsome young man who sat with his flashing dark eyes fixated on the flames. After a while, her eyes closed in spite of her efforts to keep them open. She pulled the skins over her body and fell into a dreamless sleep.

The next morning before daylight Winna came to awaken Freia. They both looked for Wiglaff, but he was nowhere to be seen. Winna gave Freia a breakfast of seeds and dried fruits. When it was clear Wiglaff was not going to return, they ran into the forest together. They planned to meet Winna's other recruits, who had been her friends from her earliest childhood. Exercises and training were the orders of the day.

***

Awakened in the darkness before dawn by the howling of a wolf, Wiglaff had grabbed a flint knife and stolen into the forest. He had a clear objective in an eagle's nest at the top of a lone pine tree. Climbing the pitchy tree at dawn, when he saw the mating pair of adult eagles fly off, he found their nest. Not disturbing the three eaglets, he collected three large tail feathers. Then he edged back down the tree and proceeded to an icy rivulet that fed the river. He laid aside his leathers and bathed in the ice-cold water, choked on all sides by a lush growth of watercress. He drank liberally and ate the peppery cress. Refreshed, he climbed out of the pool, dried in the sunshine and dressed. A stag and his doe came to drink, but they did not fear Wiglaff. Two fawns came out of hiding to join their parents at the pool.

Wiglaff walked in a pattern he had established for this time of year. At one place he stopped to dig for sassafras roots. At another, he harvested dandelions, including their greens, flowers, and roots. In a meadow, he found and collected other edible flowers, including nasturtiums and clover. He watched the bees gathering nectar and noted the direction of their flights so he could later find their hives. He gently picked up a green garter snake and let it wrap itself around his arm. He also let a female green praying mantis crawl on his arm while he looked for her large, white egg sack.

He had brought a bag to harvest whatever he fancied. So he filled his bag with sour onion greens, parsley, rosemary, sage, thyme, marjoram and edible mushrooms. On the edge of the meadow, he checked his traps and discovered a rat, a mouse, and three voles, which he placed alive in small pouches in his bag. It was essential to capture these animals alive, keep them separate and take them to his clearing for later use in his rituals.

Wiglaff wandered to the edge of the river. There hidden by gorse, he saw Winna's recruits in the water. Lithe and graceful swimmers, their garments were all strung out on the gorse around where he was standing. He did not bother the women but went down on the rocky shore to hunt for green frogs and newts among the stones. Finding several rock specimens and three small, gray frogs, he watched the trout swimming against the current and sunning near the bend in the river. Since he had over twenty fish drying near his forest clearing, he decided against taking more trout now. He did, however, harvest cattail roots, careful to wash the mud off thoroughly before he placed them in his bag.

Coming out of the gorse, he heard a young woman call his name, "Wiglaff, there you are, finally!" Freia waved at him while Winna frowned at her.

"Freia, have you no shame?" Winna said laughing.

Freia answered by splashing water with her foot first, then by diving back into the river from the bank. Wiglaff watched the two wrestling in the water. They were having fun, but their fun was serious training too.

He marveled that all the women had braided their hair to make it manageable while they swam and trained. Wiglaff enjoyed watching for a while.

Freia glanced his way from time to time. Then he was suddenly gone. She wondered why she felt sad not to find him watching her.

On the far shore a noisy group of blue-painted boys, who were warriors in training, ran to the water's edge. They did not realize just how young the lasses were. They thought it would be fun to scare the girls. So after stripping off all their clothes, they dove into the river and swam toward them. Winna's recruits swam downstream with the young men in hot pursuit. The contest was unequal because the girls had trained to swim and knew the way to use the river's current to their advantage. On the other hand, the boys thought they could terrorize them, if they caught them. They pulled and kicked with all their strength.

The river ultimately ended in the sea, but that was a long way to swim. Winna encouraged her recruits to pace themselves and seize the opportunity as a training exercise. Meanwhile, she remained to the rear of her swimmers in case one of the male pursuers came too close. One young man stood out among the others and thrashed close to Winna, who reversed direction and clasped him around the waist.

The young man was surprised and immensely gratified to have been seized by the swimmer he wanted most to embrace. Too late, though, he realized she could hold her breath far longer than he. He struggled to get free, but she had wrapped her legs around him and held him below the surface. Finally, he relaxed and let her go. She continued downstream while his fellow warriors-in-training hauled his exhausted body to the shore.

Winna urged her recruits to continue swimming for a while. When they had rounded the far bend in the river, she hurried them ashore. They ran in formation back up the river where they had hung their clothes on the gorse. Dried naturally during their run, they climbed into their animal skins, laughing but anxious about the danger they had incurred in their innocent swim. When the training broke up for the afternoon, Winna and Freia went to Wiglaff's clearing to report what had happened.

Wiglaff looked up from preparing a feast for his birds and heard them explain what had happened. When Winna told him how she had nearly drowned the leader, he said he was proud of her. He also stated that it would be wise to determine whether he had died and if there would be an attack coming soon. After they had thought about this for a moment, Wiglaff asked Winna whether any of the young blue warriors had recognized Freia.

Winna said, "I'm not sure, but I don't think anyone recognized her. Everything happened so fast. The attackers were too busy taking off their garments and eyeing their prizes to look closely at any of us."

"What about the young man you took under the water. Would he remember who you are?

Winna thought about that for a moment. "Wiglaff, I don't think so. For women, even one glance in a man's eyes will remain in the memory forever. For men, it's never that specific. At least that's what our mother told me."

Freia chimed in, "My mother said the same thing. My father took her one afternoon. He did not remember what happened afterward, but she did. Her father made my father understand his obligation. It was a close thing, but here I am, the man's eldest daughter as witness."

Wiglaff said nothing after this embarrassing personal revelation. Instead, he arose and built a fire. Puttering around, he said, "It may not be a good idea for you to exercise naked in the river for a while, at least in daylight."

Winna nodded her head in agreement. "We need to practice swimming at night anyway, so we'll change our routine. Right now, Freia and I will camp out with the others. Have a nice night's divination, brother!"

As the two departed, Freia kept her eyes on Wiglaff. She was disappointed he gave her no sign of encouragement. Today fifteen young men had plunged into the water to pursue her and the others. For all her attempts to flaunt her naked body at him, Wiglaff pretended he did not even know she was female and wondered how she could get his full attention. That night around the campfire, she asked Winna what she should do.

"Winna, I have a confession to make. I like your brother very much. I've tried to get his attention. Yet he won't pay any attention to me. What should I do?"

Winna laughed so hard that she had a hard time calming down. She told her assembled warriors what Freia had just said. They laughed too. When they all calmed down, Winna said, "My brother Wiglaff is not like most young men you will meet, and never will be. Soon he'll become the apprentice of a famous shaman. He'll enter a path of training that can last for decades, and will consume the rest of his life. My advice is simply to give up. A mere woman cannot compete against the forces my brother communes with. Find someone else, but not right away. If you bear children, you'll have to leave us to raise your family. Think things through. I won't judge you personally, no matter what decision you make. That goes for everyone here. Your freedom to choose your course in life is fundamental to who you are."

They sat in a circle around the fire for a long time contemplating what Winna just said. Then Winna sprang up and urged them, "Let's go for a night swim. Last one to the river has the first watch." She charged into the night with her warriors pursuing. They stripped off their clothing and dived into the black water. Chastened by the unintended results of their previous swim, no one screamed or laughed out loud. Instead, they swam upstream and downstream together, hoping they would not be attacked again.

On the riverbanks, insects and frogs sang. A quarter moon shone in the heavens. On her back in the water looking up at the starry sky, Winna considered what she and her warriors had experienced that day. *Had we been at fault by swimming naked? Had I been overly brutal when I took my pursuer down in the water?* She remembered the young man's strength and determination. She remembered the way he felt between her thighs. She shuddered to think about what might have happened if he had not passed out.

Freia snuck away from the the group later that night. She went to the forest clearing where Wiglaff sat watching his fire. "Hello, Wiglaff."

"I thought we had an agreement, Freia. When I am in a trance, don't interrupt me."

"Are you in a trance now?" she asked.

Wiglaff shook his head. "You are incorrigible. What do you want from me?"

"I like you, Wiglaff. I want to be your friend. No, that's not quite right. I want to be your mate. What do you think about that?" She had plopped down beside him and craned her neck to look him in the eyes.

He thought about it for a while. "Freia, did you discuss this with my sister Winna?"

She pouted. "Yes, I did."

"What did she tell you?" he asked.

Freia's mouth made a moue, and she looked down at the fire. "She said you were going to become the apprentice of a famous shaman soon and follow the path to become a shaman yourself. She told me to forget my feelings for you and find another man."

Wiglaff smiled. "My sister's wise. Perhaps you should listen to her. Are you having regrets about becoming one of her warriors ... already?"

Freia shuddered. "I have no regrets. It's the perfect role for me. I was made for it. But I was also made for other things, like marriage and family. I don't want to limit myself. I want to have it all."

Wiglaff looked into the fire and said in a melancholy voice, "Sometimes we have to choose. Once we choose one path, we exclude others ..." he paused, "We also have to keep to our choices." He paused again, "Otherwise, we'll lose our way."

Now Freia was looking into the fire as if it held the key to something deep within her. "Why do I feel that with you, I can be fulfilled and be what I am at the same time?"

Wiglaff smiled ruefully. "Maybe your feeling is an illusion. I don't mean to be unkind, but you don't know anything about me. You wouldn't listen when I told you my simple rule ... to leave me alone when I'm having my visions. I'm going to study for many years. When I return, I hope to be a shaman. Are you sure you know what having a shaman as a mate would be like?"

She was not deterred. The more he spoke, the more he seemed just right for her. "I must admit, I never considered marrying a shaman. A warrior was my ideal mate ... until I met you. Now I'm confused, especially after what happened during the attack in the river today."

"Will you please explain what you mean by that? I did not swim in the river. I did not witness the attack."

Freia sighed. "There we were swimming and minding our own business. Suddenly, a horde of blue-painted men stripped off their clothing and jumped into the water. They swam right after us. We swam away to avoid them. Thanks to Winna, we escaped. She stopped fleeing to grapple with the strongest of our pursuers. If she had not overcome him, more than one of us would have been killed ... or raped and then killed." She was shaking all over at the thought of what she had said. She was visualizing as she continued, "I saw Winna turn and embrace the lead pursuer. All I could think was that I wanted to be Winna, naked with my legs wrapped around a big, strong naked man. She subdued him. I'm not sure I could have done that. It's not that I lack the ability to hold my breath under water. I'm just not sure I could kill a man in cold blood for simply wanting to enjoy me."

Wiglaff nodded. "Tell me how I can help you plan your way forward."

She rocked back with her hands on her right knee. It was a provocative pose—as she meant it to be. Not getting her intended response from Wiglaff, she put her leg down and stared at him for a while. Still, he did not respond. She huffed and stood up, brushing the dirt off her clothes. She walked back toward Winna's camp, tears slowly trailing down her face.

Out of the darkness on the other side of the fire came Winna, who had heard the entire conversation. "Well, brother, Freia's smitten with you. Now I've got to ask you the same questions she did."

"Winna, are you asking for her or for yourself?" He poked at the fire with a stick. Sparks shot up, and the fire took on new life. Wiglaff waited while his sister collected her thoughts. He was patient. He knew his sister as well as she knew him.

"I can't blame Freia for wanting to marry you, Wiglaff. I'm worried, though, about what her desire for a home and family does for her commitment to being a warrior." Winna's lips were set in a line.

Wiglaff nodded. "You heard what she said. Do you think a woman can have 'it all' in the sense Freia means it?"

Winna answered, "I'd like to think so, yes. Men seem to do it. Why shouldn't women do it too?"

"I don't know anyone who's more committed to something than you are. You believe in your path. You're successful in recruiting others to join your cause. You're a great example to your recruits. Take for example the way you handled today's attackers. Others might not have held back and gone after the lead attacker as you did. The attacker might have decided to break your neck. Did you think about that?"

"Brother, you've got a lot to learn about what happens between men and women. I saw that attacker's face when I wrapped my legs around him. He was ecstatic. He never would have killed me. Of course, he might have slapped or punched me. He might have beaten me senseless. But kill me? Never." She picked up a stick and stirred the fire. A breeze made the flames lean sideways and swell, reddening the embers.

Wiglaff smiled when he said, "Freia was jealous that for a while you had a man between your legs."

Winna nodded and confessed, "I'm jealous of me too just thinking about it." She smiled at her confession. She shook her head and looked up at her brother. "The power of mating is beyond my ken. Looking back, I'm hoping the fellow lived through the ordeal. Does that make sense? I killed many men... and women ... in battle, but at a distance. Today, close up and wrestling naked, I may have killed a young man with my knowledge of the water, and my bare hands and legs."

Wiglaff said, "You also wrestled naked with Freia today. How did you feel about that?"

Her brother always had a way of seeing events from many perspectives. Winna told herself she should've seen the question coming. "Wiglaff, wrestling is an intimate form of communication. Today Freia learned her strength was not equal to mine. Each of my warriors learns that. I'll remain their leader only as long as I'm stronger and smarter than they are, individually and collectively."

Wiglaff observed, "I don't think you've answered my question." The two stirred the fire from either side. "If it will help, I find the image of a drowning man between a beautiful and powerful woman's legs unmanning. In fact, it's the emblem of the death of a shaman. If I succumbed to sex, I think I'd lose my powers of envisioning. I'd no longer be worthy of the shamanistic role. I may learn differently in time, but that's the way I see things now."

Winna made a sad face and said, "Wiglaff, I need to be able to talk with a person who is capable of responding. A warm body to hold me. I think I need it more than you or any man. I've often said to our mother that no one who's not at least as strong as our father will do as my mate. The young man I almost drowned today was unworthy because I overcame him. I suppose, Freia was unworthy for the same reason. Yet I'm afraid I might have killed him. I'm also afraid I might lose Freia, one of my finest recruits, to forces raging beyond my control."

"For women, marriage and a family are powerful forces. They are just a valid as any other force." Wiglaff made this observation looking directly into Winna's eyes.

Winna did not flinch when she replied, "I have my path. You know that better than anyone else. If I don't stick to my plan, we'll all die or be enslaved. I'm sure you understand."

Wiglaff said, "I do. I also understand my sister's heart is larger than her conviction." He waited until this sank in. She shuddered as she recognized the truth of what he was telling her. By way of elaboration, he said, "I've been envisioning again. My latest visions are about you. Do you want to know about them?"

Winna's eyes widened as she answered, "I only want the outlines, not the details. I want to know that my path will bear fruit. I want to know I will be victorious over our enemies. I want to know I'll achieve my dreams before I die."

Wiglaff said softly, "All these I saw." Then he was silent while Winna, the greatest future female warrior of her age, wept quietly, grateful for her brother's positive visions. When she stopped weeping, she rose, and without looking directly at Wiglaff, walked into the dark towards her camp.

Wiglaff spent the rest of the night envisioning the fate of the young man Winna had tried to drown. The blue-painted attacker, whose name was Baldur according to his visions, had recovered, but the experience of nearly drowning had changed him. He desperately wanted to ravish the one who had almost caused his death. Yet, he hated her too because she had subdued him. If only to redeem himself to his companions, Baldur boasted he would find the river lass and rape her. If she was compliant, he would force her to become his wife. If she was not compliant, he bragged he would stick her on a spit and roast her over fire.

Wiglaff decided Baldur would never get the chance for the revenge he wanted. Until his plan was firm and fully envisioned in his own mind, Wiglaff remained silent. He resolved that not even his dear sister Winna would know the outcome of his plan until it had transpired. The essence of his idea was a combination of guile and subterfuge.

***

Wiglaff asked Winna to let him borrow Freia because she knew the village customs on the other side of the river. When she said yes, Freia and he both wore blue paint. She artfully tangled her hair as it was when they first met. Wiglaff posed as Freia's witless brother and bodyguard. They went from village to village asking about the whereabouts of her father, who had been missing since the skirmishes.

As they walked from one village to another, Freia saw many of her relatives, who marveled she was still alive after what had become of her village. Distant cousins gave her hospitality and introduced her and her 'brother' to the other villagers. In the course of these meetings, she made connections with potential recruits for the women warriors. Her 'brother' searched for the boastful warrior Baldur whom he had envisioned. Under their garments, the pair carried flint knives.

At the third village they visited, they found Baldur haranguing his companions to go back to the river to find the nymphs who bathed naked. He was graphically stating what he intended to do to the lass who had placed him right where he wanted to be—between her shapely legs. They all laughed and encouraged him. Wiglaff stayed on the outside of the merriment until he artfully caught Baldur's eye. The blue painted warrior in training walked over to see what the visitor wanted.

"I've been waiting to meet the attacker who almost died trying to rape my sister in the river. Can you help me find him?" Wiglaff said this expecting Baldur to take full credit. Instead, he looked suspiciously at Wiglaff.

Circumspectly with one eyebrow raised, Baldur said, "I can find him. Why do you want to meet him?"

Wiglaff dissembled, "My sister was so impressed that she wants to marry him and repeat what she did to him in the water, only this time on land."

With a broad smile, the blue-painted Baldur confessed, "I'm the one who grappled with your sister. She had her legs wrapped around me. I knew she loved me by the way she clung to me. She was rubbing herself all over me." He winked at Wiglaff as if he would surely understand what he meant. "Since she wants a re-match on land, name the place and time. I'll be there. We'll couple all night and see where things lie in the morning." Looking back at his fellow warriors, Baldur winked, puffing out his chest.

Wiglaff smiled wryly to draw him out and said, "The time is midnight tonight. The place is right across the river from where you first saw her, in the gorse along the bank. Leave your clothes on this side of the river. You can pick them up when you swim back. I'll stand on the opposite bank with a pine torch to show you the way."

Baldur was overjoyed by the thought of possessing the lady of the river that very night. He immediately began planning for their meeting. Meanwhile, Wiglaff and Freia made their way back through the villages and crossed the river, in plenty of time to prepare for Baldur's arrival.

That evening in his clearing Wiglaff, who was no longer wearing blue paint, thanked Freia for her help. "I hope you were able to make contact with potential recruits."

She nodded. "I've found ten candidates. We'll be meeting Winna in a fortnight at dusk at an appointed place on the other side of the river. What are you planning for Baldur this midnight?"

Wiglaff replied with a stern expression, "I'm going to give the braggart and would-be rapist exactly what he deserves."

"You don't intend to kill him, do you? After all, he's my distant cousin." Freia was genuinely concerned.

Wiglaff said, "Worse punishments than death can serve to deter the man from even thinking about raping Winna. Don't worry. You'll see."

Well before midnight, Wiglaff went to his family's hut and asked his mother for a pot of pitch. His father Mordru overheard his request and asked why he needed the pitch. In as few words as possible, Wiglaff said, "I want to pay back a blue-painted warrior for trying to rape Winna in the river today."

Mordru became incensed and told his eldest son, "Just wait a few minutes while I arouse a watch team." This was exactly the response Wiglaff had anticipated from his father.

With torches and knives, the watch team accompanied Wiglaff to the place of the rendezvous. Mordru asked his men to stand well back of the agreed upon place and come when he called. He and Wiglaff took positions inside and in front of the gorse hiding place where Wiglaff had found Freia. Wiglaff stood in front of the place waving a pine torch to show Baldur the way. Mordru hid inside the gorse, where in Wiglaff's ruse, Winna should have been.

Baldur swam naked across the river as planned. He met Wiglaff and asked where the naked woman of the river was lying. Wiglaff pointed to the place where Mordru was hiding. But he asked Baldur to recount in a loud, clear voice what happened in the river one more time. Under his breath, he suggested to Baldur that the story would raise his sister's ardor to a fever's pitch. Baldur did not hesitate.

"I pursued the lass. I grabbed her in the river. I would have enjoyed her immediately except I swallowed too much water and passed out. All I could think about was ravishing her. Now can I go to her?" Baldur was clearly excited and eager to begin his night of lust.

Wiglaff did not have to answer him because Mordru came storming out of the gorse with his flint knife at the ready calling his watch team forward. Caught in the act of confessing to attempted rape, Baldur wept and groveled before the father of his intended victim. His words were useless.

Mordru asked Wiglaff to apply the pine pitch to Baldur's bare back and arse. When Wiglaff had done this, his father seized the torch and lowered it to set the pitch on fire. On fire, Baldur ran screaming to the river, his flames trailing behind him. He plunged into the water to douse the painful flames. Mordru and his men laughed uproariously while Wiglaff nodded at the justice that had been served.

When Baldur reached the opposite bank, Mordru called out across the water, "If you give one more thought to ravishing my daughter, you'll never use your manhood again. That's because I'll cut your balls off! Do you hear me?"

In a murmur, Baldur replied, "Yes, I hear you."

"Speak louder!" Mordru shouted.

Baldur bellowed, "I hear you!"

Mordru was satisfied. He told his men to return to the village and get back to bed. To Wiglaff he said, "I'm glad we were able to handle this matter. Tell me, what would you have done if I hadn't come with the others?"

"Father, it frankly had not occurred to me what might happen otherwise. Fortunately, you came and took care of the situation." This exasperated Mordru, who shook his head and waved his right hand dismissively at his useless son.

"Give me that torch, Wiglaff. I'm going back to the hut. Are you coming too?"

"No, Father. I'll be in the clearing. Say hello to Mother for me."

Mordru stomped off with the torch. Wiglaff made his way through the darkness to his clearing. He heard an owl hoot and answered it. When he arrived at his place, he found Freia waiting for him. She had followed the group to the riverside and witnessed the rough justice first hand.

"I'm glad you and your father didn't kill Baldur."

"We certainly didn't want to start another skirmish. This way, the man whose mind was devising a worse crime than attempted rape has been served a lesson. If he wants to tell his companions what happened tonight, he'll become a laughing stock. If he tries to get revenge, he knows the outcome will unman him. I hope you're not bothered by our rough form of justice."

She smiled shyly and shook her head. "Baldur needed a lesson he wouldn't forget. He'll want vengeance against you for tricking him, but he's not liable to cross the river to get it." She stepped forward and hugged Wiglaff. Stepping back, she appraised him for a moment and walked off toward Winna's camp.

Winna walked out of the shadows when Freia had disappeared. "I suppose you weren't going to tell me what happened, Wiglaff?" She asked disappointed to have been left in the dark.

"I swore I wouldn't tell you until the end was certain. Your knowing was inevitable. What do you think?"

"I should be grateful for what you and Father did, but I can handle myself. I proved that in the river." Winna still felt she could handle whatever came her way.

Wiglaff said, "We can't have naked rapists running rampant. A man like Baldur would attack any young girl he thought was vulnerable and unprotected. Now he'll think twice before he attacks another of our women. You know how strong and capable you and your women warriors are, but not all our women are warriors ... at least not yet. Do you see what I mean?"

"Regretfully, I do see what you mean. I must be getting back to my warriors. By now Freia has told the tale of the midnight festivities. I'll have to calm everyone down and quell any rumors." She hugged Wiglaff stiffly and strode off to her camp.

Wiglaff built a fire and listened to the night while he watched the flickering flames. He saw the red eyes of rabbits watching him at a distance. He heard the night sounds of humming and chirping as nature's creatures called to their prospective mates. Tired from his day's activities, the would-be shaman finally lay on his bearskin and pulled the leather covers over his body. He slept until dawn with the image of Baldur in flames recurring in his dreams.

Onna came to her son the next morning with a breakfast of seeds pressed together with honey and dried fruits. They were, she said, his reward for protecting his sister's honor. Mordru had told Onna the whole story, peppering it with curses for his worthless son and high praise for his chaste warrior daughter. Of course, he had taken all the credit for routing the would-be rapist.

Wiglaff's mother laughed with him as they reviewed what happened. She had heard the story twice—from her husband and her daughter, but now she heard the whole story again from Wiglaff, who had actually planned and executed it.

Finally satisfied that she had learned everything about the midnight surprise for Baldur, she changed the subject. "I thought you'd like to know the shaman may be making a special trip down from his mountain cavern to visit you. That means he's accepted you as his apprentice. Congratulations."

"Thank you, Mother. I know he is an old family friend. Is there anything special I should say or do when he comes?"

Onna shook her head and advised, "Just be yourself. This man knows falseness immediately. He'll know if you don't believe what you say. He doesn't care that you don't know much. Your ignorance is why he's accepted you as his student. He told me that."

When Onna left, Wiglaff thought deeply about his next steps. *I know the shaman's path is right for me ... but I have no idea what my teacher is going to require of me. Will I measure up to Master's expectations? Will I be a disappointment to Mother? I know I'm nothing but a disappointment to Father. Last night was typical ... Father is so blinded by his attitude toward me that he can't or won't recognize my contributions. Is it wrong for me to trick him into joining my plan against Baldur? I'm sure it couldn't have happened in any other way.*

Winna dropped by his clearing. "Hello, Wiglaff. I just dropped by to offer my congratulations. I understand the shaman is coming to visit. Also, I want to thank you again for defending my honor ... isn't it funny how our father took all the credit for having bested Baldur?" Wiglaff laughed with her. "I suppose the word is getting out about what happened."

"Yes. Freia, as we predicted, told the recruits what she had seen last night. They were all impressed that Father and you held a woman's honor in such esteem. Funny how it seems that they also deeply resent the over-protectiveness the men show toward them. To tell the truth, we all like to think we do not need male protection."

"Would they have wanted us to do nothing?"

"No. They were comforted by what happened. They now know that powerful men are watching over them even when they least realize it. You might say that pride has been tempered by reality."

Freia walked up while Winna was saying goodbye to Wiglaff. She said, "I'm going to the other side of the river to rally my candidates and prepare them for the big meeting." She was again dressed in blue paint for the occasion, with twigs and flowers in her tangled hair.

Wiglaff told Winna, "It looks like the wild child is well on her way to becoming a woman warrior. She carries herself proudly and walks with a touch of your swagger."

Looking down at her feet Freia said, "I guess it's goodbye, for now, Wiglaff. Knowing you is a constant education. I won't forget about the edible mushrooms. Who knows? In another decade or two when you've graduated and become a real shaman, we'll rethink our plans together."

Wiglaff smiled without commenting on her suggestion. Instead, he said, "Freia, for now, your focus has to be on helping Winna form the women warriors on both sides of the river. My focus will be on mastering the mysteries of shamanism. Good luck to us both, and goodbye to you for now."

Wiglaff watched Winna and Freia walk toward the river. A crow descended and alighted on Wiglaff's shoulder. It allowed him to stroke its beak. The bird cawed, and Wiglaff cawed in return. A dialog between the young man and the bird began, and the bird took off toward the river afterward. With the help from his birds, Wiglaff would keep watch over the wild child turning woman warrior. She was transforming, but her unique work had truly just begun.

Chapter Three

Sea Quest

"The earliest written record of a formal connection between Rome and Scotland is the attendance of the "King of Orkney" who was one of 11 British kings who submitted to the Emperor Claudius at Colchester in AD 43 following the invasion of southern Britain three months earlier. The long distances and short period of time involved strongly suggest a prior connection between Rome and Orkney, although no evidence of this has been found and the contrast with later Caledonian resistance is striking. Originals of On the Ocean do not survive, but copies are known to have existed in the 1st century so at the least a rudimentary knowledge of the geography of north Britain would have been available to Roman military intelligence. Pomponius Mela, the Roman geographer, recorded in his De Chorographia, written around AD 43, that there were 30 Orkney islands and seven Haemodae (possibly Shetland). There is certainly evidence of an Orcadian connection with Rome prior to AD 60 from pottery found at the broch of Gurness."

—https://en.wikipedia.org/wiki/Scotland_during_the_Roman_Empire

THE planned meeting between Ugard the shaman and Wiglaff had to be deferred indefinitely. Mordru rallied Onna and his children for an urgent journey straight across Caledonia. Wiglaff's earliest memories of his extended family came as a result of this journey.

Plans for their trip overland to the northern sea were made only two weeks in advance. The occasion of their departure was the capture and interrogation of a pair of Roman surveyors. From these captives, they learned about Roman imperial designs to construct a military highway. The road was to run northwest across Caledonia from the wall made in the time of Emperor Hadrian through the main northwest path but at the time not all the way to the distant northern sea.

A military highway meant that the Romans had a long-range plan to conquer Caledonia. Mordru explained that Roman intelligence had circumnavigated Britannia already. The land survey was the next piece of their strategy for conquest. Wiglaff's family decided upon a counter-plan to combat the invaders. The warriors would attack while retreating, avoiding a direct battle yet harrying the advancing Roman troops continually. Before the Romans attacked, though, the Caledonians would send their aged, women, and children ahead to the north along an escape route extending north as far as the sea. The route followed a line of villages amongst which Mordru's eight brothers had migrated in their youth to prepare for just this eventuality.

At each village, Wiglaff's family stayed for a few days. They became reacquainted with their uncles' families. They also came to know their cousins among the northern clans and tribes. They also learned about local troubles. Occasionally, they participated in skirmishes to demonstrate their unity and prowess in battle and to become accustomed to fighting alongside their relatives.

Wiglaff had no idea so many people looked like members of his own family. Wherever they went, bonds of kinship were quickly affirmed or reaffirmed. Onna 's five sisters were among the women who had married Mordru's brothers. Her family and their clan's connections were essential for the evacuation plan to work. Each household living in the host villages provided living spaces and provisions to support family members who were forced to evacuate. Cousins were exchanged from time to time to keep communication active. This helped cross-train the warriors and unified the women.

Wiglaff and Winna were anomalous among their many cousins. From the age of ten, Wiglaff had been a loner, not a convivial warrior. Winna, at nine, was a fighter, not a shy maiden waiting for a husband. Wiglaff became known as a strange boy, always daydreaming yet skilled in arts no one, not even his parents understood. For example, he could become invisible in the forest. Playing hide-and-seek, none of the cousins was better at hiding or finding others than Wiglaff. He could vanish into thin air in the middle of a village. Only Winna could find him then.

As they progressed, Winna took stock of the warriors in each village, measuring each man against her father and finding all of them wanting. As they traveled north, Mordru grew in his daughter's esteem. He also proved he was the best soldier of his clan and tribe. With each of Wiglaff's uncles, he participated in raiding ventures for which he was the leader and bravest participant. He knew how to marshal men and to lead from the front. He was strong and savage, fearless and tireless. Where others were squeamish, Mordru was bold. He could raise the spirits of his fellow warriors even while fighting against their most daunting adversaries.

One evening after Mordru had returned from a successful raid, Wiglaff heard Onna ask him about the results. "Mordru, it's good you won today. Won't your victory deter your opponents from ever allying with us in the future?"

He squinted at his wife and replied, "We'll ally only with the strong, and on our terms. Today we taught another clan not to trifle with us. Respect and fear will bring them into our alliance at the right time. For now, their opposition to us will keep them fit and trim. We did not burn their villages or kill their women and children. We only harmed the aggressors and put them to flight." He smiled as he continued, "They'll sue for an alliance against the Romans, mark my words."

Wiglaff noticed how his sister Winna was listening to their fathers' every word. The next day she seemed to stand taller than the day before. Pressing her advantage while playing with her cousins, she demonstrated that she was her father's child: Winna went hunting and shot a deer through the heart with her arrow and took it back on her shoulders to the village for rendering. It was otherwise with her brother.

Instead of hunting, Wiglaff disappeared into the forest to commune with the natural creatures and gather edible mushrooms. While Wiglaff was listening for birds, he discovered three enemy clansmen plotting against the village where his family was lodging. It became clear from their speech that the men were in league with the Romans. Wiglaff remained invisible to the plotters. When he had heard enough, he made his way quickly and silently back to the village to inform his father. Mordru listened to his son's report with increasing wrath. When he asked questions about the appearance of the three men, Wiglaff described them in minute detail and told his father he could lead a force to the very place where the three men were situated.

Mordru told his brother Baldon about the plot. They gathered an armed force of twenty young warriors and set right out with Wiglaff leading them to their prey. They surrounded the three men and moved in to take them prisoner. Confronted with their own words, the men confessed their plot and begged for forgiveness.

"Traitors," Mordru said, "You would sacrifice members of your tribe for foreign slavery!"

The leader of the three cried out, "The Romans are unbeatable. When they come through, the only survivors among us will be those who helped them achieve their goals."

Mordru replied, "You are much deceived on two points, traitor. First, the Romans will not win against us if we stay united and fight together. Second, they'll enslave or kill every one of us, no matter what they promise in advance. Do you have anything further to say before you die?"

The leader said with a sneer, "Nothing you can do to us will change the outcome. The Romans have already surveyed the distant northern shores. They're conducting a survey to build a military road that cuts straight across Caledonia. Their slaves are already mining tin and gold in Britannia. The Empire has infinite resources and men. By killing us, you sever the only hope our people have to keep to their grand plan."

Mordru smiled knowingly. "You've sealed your own destiny. Now die!" With his flint knife, he rapidly slashed the throats of each of the three prisoners. Wiglaff witnessed the executions and retched. His father shook his head in dismay at his son's squeamishness. "Brother Baldon, let's get these corpses below the ground right away. We'll let my son arrange the burial site, so it will never be found. He's at least as good at that as he is at spying."

When the bodies had been buried, Wiglaff remained to brush over the traces so that no one would ever discover the burial place. The others returned to Baldon's village, satisfied that their job was done for the day.

While Wiglaff worked, he dwelled on what the leader of the traitors said. The Romans had scouted the northern shores, yet they were going to conquer Caledonia by land. They were already working mines deep in Britannia with slaves. Wiglaff mused upon the power and resources of the Roman Empire.

How could his family help to repel their advances and stop their plan before it started in earnest? He had just finished rearranging the landscape when Winna appeared.

"I must have missed the action," she said to no one in particular as she looked around the area.

Wiglaff nodded, "Yes, but you didn't miss much. After they confessed their crime, our father slew the three traitors with his knife. They're now buried and will soon be forgotten."

"Death to traitors!" Winna said approvingly. Then she noticed her brother seemed preoccupied. "What are you thinking?"

Wiglaff hesitated for a moment and said, "I've been thinking about what the lead traitor said."

Winna was intrigued. "So what did he say?"

"He talked about a grand plan of Rome to conquer our country. They'll come by land and push straight to the sea along the route we're taking now. They've already surveyed the northern shore by ship."

Winna pondered what her brother said. "How did the traitors communicate with the Romans?"

Wiglaff answered, "The leader said that by killing him, the communication link would be severed."

"That's well, brother. Our father was right to dispatch him. I only wish I'd been here to see justice done. What's the matter? You look green. Are you sick?"

"I was sick at the sight of the bloodshed. The three men had their throats sliced. They bled out on the ground, twitching and gurgling."

Winna smiled and shook her head. She never had trouble with the sight of blood when it had been shed for justice. She shrugged and said, "My deer is being dressed by our mother. I drank the creature's blood. We'll have venison for dinner

tonight. If you hurry, you can have the raw heart and liver."
She knew he liked those parts of the deer best of all.

Wiglaff smiled and said, "I'm going to walk the forest
until evening. It's mushroom season. After finding the three
traitors while seeking mushrooms this morning, I don't know
what else I'll discover. If anyone asks about me, tell them I'll
be back for dinner." The boy walked into the forest and
disappeared. Winna scoured the area where she had found
her brother. She had to admit that Wiglaff had done well. She
would not know how to find the three bodies that were
supposedly buried there.

Wiglaff did not go far before he found a family of wild
boars rooting around an ancient oak tree. He did not disturb
them but watched where they were foraging. When the boars
trotted off, he dug around the roots of the tree and found the
mushrooms they were seeking. He placed them in his leather
pouch with the other edibles he had found that morning.
Walking deeper into the woods, he heard men tramping
nearby. They were trying to whisper, but Wiglaff heard every
word they said.

One remarked, "He has to be around here somewhere.
Did you see how he retched when his father slew those three
traitors?"

His companion answered with a raucous laugh, "He's no
warrior. That's for certain. He's strange. What should we do to
him when we find him?"

A third young man said, "We'll beat him and hang him
upside down from a tree limb. That's what a coward like him
deserves."

Wiglaff slipped silently up the branches of a maple tree
and watched from above as five men futilely searched for him.
He memorized the faces of his supposed extended family.

Winna appeared suddenly and asked the men, "What are you looking for? The traitors have been killed."

The leader of the group said, "We're looking for your cowardly brother Wiglaff. He got sick when your father killed those men today. We're going to teach him a lesson."

Winna smiled. "Give up. You'll never find him unless he wants you to."

"What are you saying? Perhaps we should teach the lesson to you instead." He looked at his brothers-in-arms with a wink. "Or maybe we have other lessons for you. Since you're here, we'll start with you. Later we'll deal with him."

Wiglaff was about to reveal his position to protect his sister, but she drew her knives, one in each hand and crouched. "Who's first?" she asked, threatening.

The leader stepped forward and signaled the others to stand back while he handled the girl. Wiglaff knew the young man was making a huge mistake, but there was nothing he could do. When the man stood an arm's length from Winna, she attacked, slicing his knife's sheath from his belt and opening his deerskin garment from his neck to his waist. She then sheathed her knives and gripped the man's arm behind him. Propelling him forward headfirst, she rammed his head into the trunk of the tree in which Wiglaff was hiding.

Noticing that the leader had passed out on the ground, Winna wheeled to see what the other four men intended. They were bewildered because their leader had been defeated by a mere girl. She advanced a few steps, and then she feinted as if she were going to charge the four. They fled in all directions. She laughed with her hands on her hips, relieved not to have to do harm but still aching for action.

She cupped her hand to her mouth and said, "Brother Wiglaff, if you can hear me, come out and truss this braggart. Do whatever you want with him. I've got to get back to help

Mother with dinner." She picked up the man's knife and sheath and dropped a deer hide rope on the man's body. Then she ran off in the direction of the village.

Wiglaff climbed down from the tree and used Winna's deer-hide rope to tie up and hoist the man upside-down from a broad maple branch. When the man revived and discovered himself hanging by his feet, he began to scream. Wiglaff ignored him and continued his search for mushrooms, this time circling back toward the village.

It was dark when he entered the compound. At its center burned a great fire with deer parts on stakes roasting around it. Wiglaff saw the deer's hide stretched between two trees, drying. He saw the stag's head on a pole, its antlers reaching high into the darkness. The warriors were sitting in a circle around the fire telling stories.

Winna saw Wiglaff and fetched him a parcel containing the deer's raw heart and liver. She used her knife to share the organs with her brother. Boldon asked the assemblage where his son and his four companions were, but no one had an answer. Wiglaff and Winna slipped back into the shadows as the five missing men approached the fire with a wild story about their being attacked by an overwhelming force of enemy clansmen in the woods. Boldon was about to round up a band of his own men to seek revenge when Winna stepped out of the shadows.

"There is no need for action. Before anyone gives the alarm," she exclaimed, "these young men should tell the truth about what really happened in the woods."

Boldon's son stood by his lie about an overwhelming force. "I stood up to the attackers while everyone else fled. The assailants knocked me out and hung me upside down from a maple branch. My four companions cut me down, or I'd still be hanging there."

"If what you say is true, where are your knife and sheath?" Winna asked innocently.

The young warrior grabbed at his side and found his knife was missing.

Mordru narrowed his eyes. "That's a good question. Answer it."

Now Winna was holding up the sheath with the knife tucked inside. "Is this, perhaps, what you're looking for?"

The man scowled and lunged for his knife, but Winna tossed it to Wiglaff, who caught it and said, "These five men tried to find me to teach me a lesson. They were about to do harm to my sister, but she defeated the leader and disarmed him. Winna bashed his head against a maple tree and knocked him out. When she looked around, the other four fled. I'm the one who strung this man from the maple bough."

Mordru was now laughing uncontrollably. His brother Boldon was seething with rage at his son's defeat and humiliation at the hands of the girl and her brother.

"Relax, Boldon," Mordru counseled. "These two can do such things by magic. You're lucky your son and the others survived their encounter with them. In the future, I suggest you all take care to treat my eldest children with respect." He rose from the ground and used his knife to cut a piece of venison from the piece of carcass nearest to the fire.

Boldon saw that his son was looking daggers at Winna. "Bordon, stand down. You've been bested by a girl. You're disgraced. Live with it. You're lucky she didn't kill you. We're all lucky since that would have started a blood feud within our family. As for your companions' flight, you'll have to stiffen their spines or find better friends. Tomorrow morning, I'll have you five doing exercises that will test your endurance. We've got to defeat the Romans. We aren't going to do that if you can't even handle children in our own family." He rose and carved out a piece of venison and ate it next to Mordru while they discussed strategy.

"Boldon, what did the leader of those traitors mean when he talked of mines being worked with slaves in Britannia?" Mordru asked.

"You'll discover in the north country that Roman engineers have landed at various places on the coast to search for gold and silver, tin and lead. They travel with their slaves, but they also take prisoners among our people and work them as slaves in their excavations too."

"They must have found signs of what they've been looking for. That would provide the justification for their military plans for conquest." Mordru frowned. "We've been so focused on keeping them south of their wall, we didn't think about their taking other approaches from the north and, particularly, from the sea. I could kick myself for not thinking about that."

While they continued their dialog, their wives, Onna and Fria, were discussing sustenance and provisions in Boldon and Fria's hut.

"Onna, we will give shelter to your family whenever you need to come here. Our forests are rich in game and our lakes and streams crowded with fish. We have an excellent harvest of oats once a year and our woods and fields are full of nuts and berries. We have plenty of water for drinking and bathing. If you'll only bring hides and skins, you'll have all the warmth you'll need to last through the winter."

"Fria, you're most generous. If we have to flee to the north, we'll be coming on the route we're taking now. We should be sure that we can supply our men with arms—arrows and spears, mainly, so they can attack as they flee. We must also plan to fashion hiding places from which to attack. My Winna wants to identify girls like herself who what to be warriors. There won't be many of those, but we should make sure they're acquainted with one another, just in case."

The women talked about practical matters, including the creation of lethal poisons. "My son Wiglaff is becoming an expert on poisonous mushrooms. He knows the edible kinds from the deadly ones. Tonight he brought me truffles, the mushrooms that grow amid the roots of giant oak trees. He saw boars feasting on them and harvested what they left behind. In spring he finds the morels with their sponge-like heads and hollow centers. He has found in our woods the same mushroom that reputedly killed the Roman Emperor Claudius. He's also interested in an orange-capped mushroom that, in the right measure, gives him visions."

"Your son is gifted with second sight. That can be worth more than legions in the field. It could be our critical advantage in war. How will you keep him from dying in the skirmishes?"

"Wiglaff is, as you say, gifted. His father is both disgusted that he isn't a warrior like him and proud that he's making his own way. From his earliest days, he's been sensitive and aware. One day, I feel, he'll save our people from ruin. His sister, a born warrior, is his shield against his father's wrath at his supposed weakness. Then too, he proves his worth as he did today as a spy. And his sister's reputation as a warrior has to be tempered since her effectiveness must be balanced by her invisibility. It's going to be important for the Romans to underestimate what women can do in our defense. That worked in Britannia with Boadicea. It will work here in Caledonia as well."

The women continued to deliberate until late at night. As they did so, Wiglaff and Winna crawled into the bear skins on the hut's floor and slept until daylight when Mordru ordered the family to continue north as they had planned. Boldon and his family, including Boldor and his friends, waved goodbye. From over his shoulder, Wiglaff heard Boldon shouting orders. The promised rigorous training exercises for Boldor and his friends had begun.

As they progressed, Wiglaff took point position ahead of the others. He was, therefore, first to scout their route. Winna followed her brother and, when she could, shot game for their food. Each night they ate venison, rabbit or boar. Sometimes they ate fish. Wiglaff was adept at tickling trout at the bends of rills.

Onna prepared the family's meals by supplementing the fresh game with nuts, grains, and berries they foraged along the way. The green hills and blue skies were the paradise they loved. Rains fell daily in the early afternoon, and the smell of the earth after the rain was like a new beginning. Dramatic clouds piled up while the sunshine's rays pierced through and illuminated features of the hills and valleys of the rough north country.

Wiglaff rarely stayed in the villages where the others slept at night. Instead, he haunted the forests and searched for outlying areas where discoveries could be made. He caught mice and rats and ate their hearts and livers. He sought the nests of birds and collected rare feathers. He kept his eyes and ears open while he was awake. So it was that he first noticed a band of enemy tribesmen following a path in parallel to his family's track.

Wiglaff swiftly reported the massing of men in the east. These warriors were evidently going to intercept the family's passage through the upcoming foothills. Mordru asked his son for more information. Wiglaff told his father they would be slaughtered if they continued into the pass as they had planned. Mordru's immediate impulse was to charge the enemy's emplacement and destroy them before they could attack. Wiglaff had thought about that strategy and realized it would not work.

"Father, they are too many. We are too few. We must use stealth instead of brawn this time." This admonition filled both Mordru and Winna with loathing. As warriors, they wanted to take action, not evasion. Still, they understood and agreed with Wiglaff when he suggested, "Let's use the power of stealth to hobble our adversaries."

When Mordru was ready to hear more, Wiglaff continued, "Why not use our poisons to our advantage?" This pleased Winna though Mordru was still not convinced.

The next day, Winna shot three laggards among the enemy force with poisoned arrows. They died horribly, screaming in agony. Winna's arrows had been well-placed, but their enemy had no idea who had shot them. Such was the demoralization of the enemy that they abandoned their plan to attack the family in the foothills. Instead, they opted to hide and wait in an encampment while they sent out scouts.

Winna's arrows wounded the scouts, who died in agony from the poison. Winna entered the enemy camp that same night and shot the guards with poisoned arrows. In the meantime, the family made it through the pass. The enemy numbers began to swell because the threatened troops had called for reinforcements.

Mordru was incensed, but his wife and children counseled patience. They suggested that he should attack the camp of the enemy by night. Mordru felt energized by the idea and honed his weapons.

At midnight, Mordru attacked, with Winna using her arrows as a safeguard. When the enemy sentries menaced her father, her arrows caused them grief. When the leader emerged from his tent, her poisoned arrows hit him in the chest and caused his horrible screams through the night.

Wiglaff watched as his father and sister cut down the enemy's leadership and after the threat had been subdued, they eliminated as many of their number as possible.

"Too bad," Mordru said the next morning as he reflected on his victory of the previous night, "we laid low so many who might have been our allies against the Romans."

His daughter rejoined, "Yet we could never have trusted such men as we killed last night. We're rid of them now. Let's rejoice!"

Wiglaff retreated into the forest after this victory to contemplate the future. As he studied the labyrinthine design of spiders' webs, he said to himself, "Patterns define nature. They also define humans. The pattern I see is more combat as we go north. Vigilance will help, and our watchfulness will be richly rewarded."

Mordru was well aware of the dangers as they clawed their way north, village by village. Wiglaff thought that if no humans had inhabited the land, his family would have had everything they needed. Jealousy, envy, and spite made their own tribesmen and clansmen rise against them. They continued marching north, staying at Mordru's brothers' huts, but they discovered that the more successful they were against their enemies, the more enemies sprang up against them.

Before he slew the leader of one opposing band, Mordru asked him, "Why do you come against us, you who are our kin. Don't you realize you are abetting our common enemy the Roman Empire."

The leader responded, "I must oppose what I know. The threat that I can never know, I must embrace, utterly."

This point of view was a caution to Mordru. Wiglaff and Winna understood what the leader meant, but they allowed their father to take care of their family's security. They realized he would not understand the nuances of what he had heard. His knife put an end to the lives of his captives.

By stealth, Wiglaff discovered the depth of the secret Roman infiltration from the north. Everywhere his family traveled, the Romans had made inroads. In fact, Roman spies and informers seemed to be everywhere. In some villages, Roman agents had been in place for over a hundred years. Since their agents could not use the gold and silver they had been paid for their services, they merely hid their supposed wealth in hoards in their huts. For Wiglaff and Winna, these peoples' disloyalty was evident. Mordru slew any spies they could find. Since they could not root out all the Roman agents, they continued north searching for Roman sympathizers and cutting off all who seemed to fit the treacherous mold.

Gradually the character of Mordru's family's quest changed as they continued northward. Instead of continuing to focus on their initial strategy of evacuation, they now concentrated on a dual strategy that now included the elimination of spies. They tried to identify and exterminate anyone who was in league with the Romans. Complementing this new parallel strategy was their effort to discover as much as possible about the Roman incursions along the northern coast of Caledonia.

As they were passed from one brother to another along their journey, they learned that the Romans had been busy in the north, not only along the coastline but on the offshore islands. They encountered evidence of recent Roman contact in villages. Mordru's brothers were able to inform him of the frequency of Roman contact and the names of people who were in league with the Romans. Fortunately, none of Mordru's brothers, their wives or their families were among the traitors. The plan when Mordru entered any village was to seek counsel with Mordru's resident brother and move expeditiously to kill the Roman contacts.

As they moved northward, they were met with increasing opposition from the Roman faction. This did not deter Mordru. Instead, he was heartened because his enemies were coming out to meeting him in battle. He preferred open combat to the game of patient waiting that was necessary for spy hunting. For that clandestine purpose, he used his otherwise useless son Wiglaff and his misfit warrior daughter Winna. At the same time, Onna carried out her own initiatives among the women to be sure her children would have refuge in times of need.

Wiglaff's independence as a lone observer was reinforced wherever his family traveled. His youthful peers hated him on sight, and they might have ostracized or killed him if he had not naturally avoided them and hidden in the forest. Pushing north, he remained in the vanguard of their travels, partially because his father felt he was expendable. What did it matter if a mere dreamer lost his life? As for Winna, she was for the male warriors, an abomination. A woman warrior could never join the men in the forward edge of combat. So her father risked her life as a scout daily. It was difficult for her to accept that her father wished her dead, but she knew her brother would never live up to his father's expectations. As for herself, Winna thought the greater the dangers she endured, the more likely her father would finally recognize her worthiness to be his heir.

Wiglaff was fishing in an icy stream clogged with watercress when he next overheard the enemy, only this time, it was a Roman agent meeting his Caledonian spy in what they thought was a secret place. Sinking under the frigid water and letting the natural cover of the watercress cover his head, Wiglaff listened carefully as the sounds carried over the water.

"What do you know about this troublemaker Mordru? He has already disrupted our operations and set back the timetable for the completion of the military highway." The Roman agent had a good but not great command of the Pictish language. There was no mistaking his venomous opinion about Wiglaff's father's activities.

The spy replied, "Mordru isn't to be trifled with. He's a great warrior, respected throughout Caledonia for his bravery in battle and his defense of his homeland. No less troubling are his two eldest children, the boy called Wiglaff and the girl Winna. He deploys these children as if they were adults. One thing more, his wife, Onna, is a separate force to reckon with. She stirs up trouble wherever she travels. She's in charge of planning and weapons … and she knows how to brew poisons."

"So why not eliminate all of them as a precaution?" the Roman agent asked him.

"That's much easier said than done," the Pict replied. "Many have tried, both inside their family and from the outside. They have a hundred tricks to foil any attempt."

The Roman hesitated a long while before he replied. "I'm paying you a lot of money to keep our secrets safe. Perhaps I should pay someone else to inform instead of you. That way, I'd get fewer excuses and better results."

"Don't you threaten me, Roman. You'll get no better results from anyone else. Besides, you'll never know when you're vulnerable. I've been working with your people for two generations. I know how to keep our activities absolutely secure. Working with any of the others, you wouldn't know who to trust. You'd be dead inside a week."

The Roman agent lashed out, saying, "I'm going to give you two days to get results. If you don't have something vital to report, I'm going to replace you. You can't threaten me. Rome will prevail whether I'm here or not. The Empire will send replacements indefinitely until our ends are met. Do you understand me?"

"Yes, I think I do. You'll get your results. Now I'll escort you back to safety. Have a drink from the stream and try some watercress. You may like the taste. It has a peppery flavor this time of year."

The Roman agent replied, "I prefer the Roman gramineae, the daily dole of heated grain porridge. It may only be herbs and grain, but it's done me good service for over thirty years. I'll drink the water gladly. There's nothing quite like it in Rome. The only thing close is the cold water brought via aqueducts from the mountains each spring."

The Roman dipped his hand into the water around five inches from Wiglaff's head, but he did not see the boy hiding under an alcove covered by the tangled greenery. Wiglaff withheld his inclination to strike the agent with his knife immediately. He wanted to discover where the agent came from. When the Roman and the Pict had wandered off, Wiglaff emerged from the stream and followed them at a distance.

At that time, the hills of northern Caledonia were thick with forests, providing ample cover for a watcher like Wiglaff. The Roman and the Pict walked a well-worn path. Wiglaff did not take their path. Instead, he walked silently through the woods, careful not to be seen or heard. He heard nothing from his prey because they were not speaking for fear of being overheard.

The walk continued throughout the afternoon, including a time of showers that soaked them all to the bone. For

Wiglaff, whose diet included raw liver, the cold, wet weather was no impediment. For the people he followed, the chill of walking in wet, clammy clothing made them visibly shiver. Wiglaff smiled at their discomfort.

At the edge of the forest, the Pict stopped and pointed to the path the Roman agent was to take over the next rise through gorse and bracken. Wiglaff noticed three watchers in the woods observing the parting of the Roman agent and the Pict. The watchers all wore blue-colored paint on their skin. When the Roman agent set out on his trek alone, the Picts withdrew.

Wiglaff followed the Roman, sheltered by the falling darkness. He suspected that at some point the Roman scouts would be set. He resolved that he would have to be careful to avoid detection. He took a calculated risk that the Roman agent was still far from his destination and Wiglaff was correct.

As it turned out, the Roman encampment was far away to the north. It occupied the top of a hill, which was fortified with sharp stakes emanating from all sides. Wiglaff had repeatedly been told that the Romans built the best forts in the world. He had also been informed that they posted watchers in special raised platforms on each side of their square structures. The Roman agent passed through a checkpoint where he gave a password. Once inside the structure, he was safe. Only when he emerged would he be vulnerable again.

Wiglaff settled down for the night in a place where he could observe the entrance to the fort without being seen. An hour before dawn, he withdrew to the edge of the forest. There he noticed the Picts had left no guards in place. As quickly as possible, Wiglaff retraced his way to the village where his family was staying. Over breakfast, he told his father what he had discovered.

Mordru was alarmed and wanted to attack the Roman camp immediately. Winna clearly wanted to take some bold action as well. Fortunately, Onna's wise counsel prevailed.

Onna said, "Satisfying as it may seem to you to lose your lives attacking our oppressors, think through your actions to take the least risk for the most reward. Husband and daughter, your dying means nothing if all our family's plans are ruined. Killing a few Romans in a distant outpost will only invite the Romans to reinforce their position. They will not regard an attack as a setback. In fact, Rome may use an attack to justify additional reinforcements and to accelerate funding their invasion."

Wiglaff wondered at his mother's counsel. He recalled that he could have killed the Roman at the stream but held back. Ironically, he had discovered more because he had not struck. He decided to ask a question that had been bothering him since he left off watching the Roman camp. "What action will the Pict take within the next few hours to satisfy the demand of his Roman agent? If he doesn't take a dramatic action that the Roman approves of, he's likely to be replaced or killed."

Mordru looked at his son for a long time, his mind evaluating what he had just heard. "As much as I hate to admit it, Wiglaff, you're correct. The Pict is our proper target right now. I'll wager he's gathering a force to cut us all down. In order to counter his attack, we'll have to pull our people together and seize him. I'll go to my brother to arrange for military action. Meanwhile, I want you to get some sleep. You've been awake all night. Winna will watch over you while you rest."

Mordru left immediately to advise his brother Wolding. An hour later, Onna and Winna heard him with the warriors leaving the village in the direction of the Pictish camp.

Wiglaff, who was used to snatching catnaps, awakened a few minutes after his father and uncle had departed. Winna advised him to continue sleeping, but Wiglaff had an odd feeling his father's men were not safe.

Wiglaff said, "Quickly, let's find somewhere to hide. Follow me with the children." The women and children followed Wiglaff out of the hut and into the forest. An ancient, gnarled tree became their refuge. When Onna and the young children were safe in the limbs of the tree, Wiglaff and Winna returned to watch the village from a distance. Not long thereafter, a Pictish raiding party entered the village from the direction opposite to Mordru's advance. They went straight to the hut where Mordru's brother Wolding dwelled. They piled brush on all sides of the structure and lit a fire. They watched the flames devour the building, but they were not satisfied because no one had been trapped inside. The Picts withdrew the same way they entered. Wiglaff and Winna followed them.

The leader of the Picts fell behind the others. He seemed to be considering what he had accomplished. Winna drew one of her poison-tipped arrows and shot him in the heart. She shot so well, the poison was not needed. Running to the dead body, she pulled out her arrow so she could use it again. She ran after the main Pictish party, selecting her targets from those who lagged behind. As she released her arrows at the backs of the troops, those in front remained oblivious of what was happening behind them. She killed eight before Wiglaff told her to stop. This was a good idea at the time since Mordru's group, returning from the Pictish camp, met the Picts Winna had followed head on. A battle ensued during which all the Picts were slain except for one, who set out at a run toward the Roman camp. Winna and Wiglaff followed the fugitive.

At the edge of the forest, the running man met three Pictish guards. He convinced them to let him continue to the Roman camp to make his report. After he was gone, Winna slew the three remaining guards with three arrows. Wiglaff pursued the fugitive to the Roman camp. He waited while the Pict entered the camp, and after an hourglass of time, a Roman squad came out with the Pict bound as a prisoner. He carried a cross. In front of their camp, the soldiers crucified the Pict. Then the Romans returned to their fort, leaving the Pict hanging on the cross. Not long afterward, the Roman agent emerged and made his way toward the Picts' camp. Wiglaff followed at a distance, and Winna followed both of them, with an arrow notched and ready in her bowstring.

That evening the Pictish women built a fire in the middle of their camp. The Roman agent talked with one of the women by the fire. Winna slipped into the camp and shot two fatal arrows respectively into the backs of the Pict and the Roman agent. Wiglaff and Winna then retreated and returned to the village where they were staying.

There Mordru and his band were telling tales around their fire. They were bragging about having routed an entire Pictish force, slaying them to the last man. Chuckling to themselves, Wiglaff and Winna went into the woods and brought Onna and the children back to the hut where they all bedded down for the night.

By daylight, Mordru and his family were on their way north again. Mordru and Winna walked together. Knowing her father's temper, she waited until just the right time to speak.

"Father, we may have trouble with the Romans now."

"Winna, why do you think so?" her father asked, his brow knit with concern.

"I killed the Roman and the Pictish woman who was his contact last night."

Mordru's eyes widened. "You didn't also happen to kill some Pictish warriors before the battle, did you?"

Winna replied, "Yes, only nine of them, but I stopped just before you, your brother, and your forces engaged them."

Mordru shook his head in wonder. "I thought our luck was too good to be true. What do you think comes next?"

Winna waved for Wiglaff to come forward. "Tell Father what you think happens next, Wiglaff."

The boy said, "The Romans crucified the Pict who told them about the death of their agent. He's hanging on a cross outside their camp as we speak. He'll be left there as an example. I don't think any Pict will collaborate with the Romans for a long while. That doesn't mean the Romans are going anywhere on account of their temporary setback. Their fort is well placed and fortified. As long as they continue to get supplies, they'll thrive."

Mordru nodded reflectively. "We could try to interrupt their supply line."

Wiglaff said, "We'd lose many warriors doing that, and the Romans might reinforce their position rather than withdraw."

"You sound just like your mother." Mordru screwed up his face in exasperation. Winna made the same face.

"Did I hear my name mentioned?" asked Onna as she tried to keep the children in line.

Mordru shook his head. "It's nothing, Onna. I suppose you're right, Wiglaff. We'll not change from our plan. We'll be overlooking the northern sea in another two weeks. Let's hope the Romans aren't thickly settling the land between here and there."

***

Mordru's eighth brother lived in a village on a hill overlooking the distant sea. Once settled in his hut, Mordru's family walked to the summit and looked out over the vast, tumultuous gray and white-specked sea. Wiglaff made out a small pier sticking out into the sea, with a Roman ship moored to the pier. Slaves were offloading provisions. Mordru's hand instinctively went to his knife. Winna felt for her arrows.

"Wiglaff and Winna, see those men working near the ship?" Mordru asked. "Those are Roman slaves. They work all day and much of the night. They do nothing unless they are told to do so. They'll probably never be free … if they ever were. That's what our people will become if we allow the Romans to conquer Caledonia." Wiglaff and Winna watched the men work. They observed the Roman overseer use his whip repeatedly when a slave fell on his knee due to the weight of his burden.

Wiglaff and Winna were impressed by the image of that slave. Mordru said, "When the Romans attack from the south, our people here will have to destroy that pier, and cut the line of supply to the Roman fort we passed. Under no circumstance can the Romans be allowed to advance on us from two directions at the same time. We'll be pressed hard enough to deal with one advancing force."

That evening by the light of the village fire, Mordru talked with his brother Forfar. "Forfar, you're going to have to tell me why you feel safe when your village is so near the Roman port."

"Mordru, we are safe as long as the Romans are not at war with us."

"Forfar, we are at war with Rome right now. Make no mistake. It only seems peaceful because we're not fighting. The Romans move slowly, yet relentlessly they come. When the time arises that they advance from the south, you're going to have to work with our northern brethren to cut them off, destroying their port and their fort. Will you do these things?"

"Aye, I'll do what I have to do, even if I end up dead," Forfar pledged.

Winna looked at her uncle wincing in the firelight. She knew he was a brave man against an unstoppable force. "So Father, when the Romans fight in the north, will Uncle Forfar's old people, the women, and the children flee to the south?"

"Yes, Winna. And at the same time the old people, the women and the children down by the wall will be fleeing north. The Romans will have an opportunity to close like pincers from both ends of Caledonia. Their plan will be to pour additional troops into our land until we're overwhelmed and enslaved or killed. You saw the slave near the ship today. That slave will be all of us if we lose." He let the image bore into her mind.

Winna brooded for a moment. Then she got a fierce look and said, "We'll never be slaves, Father! We must not let the Romans win."

Mordru laughed, "You have the fighting spirit, Winna. I wish all our people felt as brave as you are … and were as competent." He looked daggers at his son when he said this.

Winna asked, "Father, what if I could set the slave free and bring him to live with us?"

Mordru's eyes grew wide. "Winna, if you bring us the slave, we'll give him hospitality."

That night, Winna spoke with Wiglaff. Her father's judgment weighed on her mind like a military order. Wiglaff listened to his sister's plan to free the slave.

Winna said, "There are seven slaves and four soldiers near the ship. I believe I can eliminate the soldiers with my arrows. The question is, how to deal with the slaves?"

Wiglaff told her, "We've no idea whether all the slaves wish to be freed. We also don't know when the soldiers from the fort will be coming for their provisions. Finally, we don't know what we're going to be doing with the ship."

Winna thought her brother was being overly fussy. "Wiglaff, we can't solve all the problems before we act. Let's just do something. After we begin, everything will turn out fine. You'll see."

Wiglaff countered, "Winna, I don't want to see you dead before your time. Let's seek the council of our father and the others." Reluctantly, she agreed.

Wiglaff spoke before his father and his uncle. "Winna has a workable idea to free the slave we saw today. Her plan can succeed if you help us. If you don't help us, it still may succeed, but one or both of us will probably die ... for nothing. Will you help us?"

Mordru said, "I agree that you'd be taking many risks for a small reward. If you want us to help, what do you want us to do?"

Wiglaff looked at Winna before he began. "My concern is Romans coming up from the fort for the provisions that have been stacked by the pier. You and Uncle Forfar must take care of that group while we free the slaves. If the Romans don't come from the fort, you must arrange to carry the provisions to the village. Actually, you will need to do that in any case. The freed slaves can help, I think. Uncle Forfar, is anyone in your village an experienced sailor?"

"I can sail, Wiglaff. That's why I chose the village closest to the sea."

"Uncle, tonight, you're going to capture our future navy."

Mordru and Forfar laughed, but Wiglaff was not laughing with them. He was serious.

"Father, we need your leadership to make this plan work. Will you lead us?"

Mordru nodded. With Forfar and Winna, he planned the whole operation. By midnight, the plan was ready for execution. Mordru took eight men to deal with the forces from the Roman fort. Forfar took eight men to overcome the two sleeping Roman guards at the port and seize the ship. Winna's arrows would eliminate the two Romans who were defending the ship itself. Wiglaff would free the slaves and divide them into three groups. Three would sail the ship under Forfar's command. Another two would carry the provisions to the village under Winna's command. The two remaining slaves would stand by Wiglaff to join either of the two other slave groups depending on what was needed.

The attack went as planned. Winna's arrows eliminated the two Roman guards. Swiftly Forfar's men slipped into the Roman tent to kill the two sleeping soldiers. Then Forfar and his warriors cast off the lines from the ship and stood by to shove off. Wiglaff, knife in hand, freed the slaves and separated them into the three groups as planned. Two jumped on the ship and grabbed the oars. Another two began to lift the provisions and take them up the hill. Wiglaff stood on the pier with the three others watching how things were progressing. While he was doing that, the slave whom he had seen fall onto his knees earlier gestured for him to lend him his knife. Wiglaff did not hesitate, and the slave drove the flint blade into the heart of a fellow slave.

He hissed, "Vile spy!" and handed the blade back to Wiglaff.

Wiglaff gestured for the slave to join those carrying the provisions up the hill to the village. The slave eagerly obliged. By now the ship had rowed well offshore. Wiglaff and one of Forfar's men piled the bodies of the dead.

Meanwhile, Winna ran up the hill where she and Mordru's force encountered six Roman soldiers from the fort, surprising them in the night. They made quick work of their enemy, killing them all. As they were picking up the Roman soldiers' weapons, they lugged their dead bodies to the pier area before joining the others in carrying more provisions.

When all but one portion of the provisions had been relocated to Forfar's village, Mordru met the slaves on the pier. "You are free now. You have two choices. You can accept our hospitality and live with us. If you stay with us, life will be hard, but you'll be free. Or you can take your chances on your own. If you want to take your chances, so be it. Take the remainder of the provisions and the weapons and depart on the ship."

The slaves were adamant about taking their chances, except for the slave who had slain the spy. He chose to follow Mordru. His first assigned task was to help bury the dead bodies.

With a torch, Mordru signaled the ship to approach the pier and pick up the other slaves, provisions, and the arms. Then Mordru told Forfar, "Turn over the ship to the slaves and let them sail wherever they chose to go." Forfar leapt ashore while the slaves climbed aboard and rowed away.

As they walked to Forfar's hut, Mordru told him, "Tonight was practice for what you must do when you receive the signal. Under no circumstance is Rome to be allowed to press south from here."

Forfar replied, "We were lucky tonight. We foresaw the potential for the Roman soldiers' arrival from the fort. Your son and daughter had a good idea, and you planned it to perfection. Now, of course, we'll have to see what Rome will do to retaliate. It's too much to hope that they'll abandon their fort … or their beachhead. What do you think the slaves will do with the ship we just gave them?"

Mordru shook his head. "I don't know. Slaves are kept and fed like domestic animals. When they get hungry, they're liable to be back looking for handouts. If that happens, I recommend taking care of them and putting them to work. As for the slave who has chosen to follow me, I'll keep him close and use his knowledge of the Romans to help our cause. We'll be leaving in the morning. Thanks for your hospitality. I'm hoping we won't have to impose on you again for a very long time."

"Brother, you are most welcome to come anytime. It's good to see family occasionally. Living at the far end of Caledonia, I get lonely looking at the cold and dreary sea."

Mordru bade his brother's family goodbye at dawn. Wiglaff took point and served as the lead scout. Winna walked in parallel to the east. Onna and the children followed Mordru. Festus, the former slave, carried Onna's provisions and played guessing games with the children while they walked.

***

The journey home was less an adventure than an obligation. The family retraced their path, village by village. Mordru told his brothers stories of his exploits going north. He warned that Forfar might need reinforcements if the Romans decided to bolster their activities at the fort and port on the seacoast.

Wiglaff and Festus struck up a friendship, the earliest fruit of which was Wiglaff's honing his Latin language skills. In return, Wiglaff taught Festus how to select edible mushrooms. Winna kept away from Festus because of the way he eyed her. She was a huntress, and she instinctively avoided men in general, except for her father and her brother Wiglaff.

The long anticipated return of Mordru and his family was celebrated with an enormous bonfire with spits of roast venison and roasted wild boar. The family had been gone for over a year and the tales they spun kept the villagers entertained for hours.

Meanwhile, Wiglaff and Winna returned to their beloved forest. Festus became Onna's primary household helper. The former slave was much too practical to spend much time in the woods. Still, Wiglaff liked Festus to spend an hourglass a day with him for conversation in Latin. Thus it was that the freed slave confided to Wiglaff that before he was enslaved, he had been a schoolteacher in Rome. His enslavement resulted from his having written a satire on the Emperor, which Wiglaff committed to memory.

To Mordru's mortification and Wiglaff's delight, the slave became the tutor for all Onna's children. Eventually, he became the schoolmaster for the entire village. Even Winna became Festus's student for a while. He taught her martial vocabulary and much about the Roman gods of war. He also taught her how to write official letters.

Only Mordru refused to learn from Festus. Perhaps he did not want to pollute his mind with thoughts from the hated enemy. More likely, he was afraid the schoolmaster would disrespect him for his ignorance. Yet Festus was smart enough to know he could be of service to his benefactor as a translator and scribe. Patient and careful, the schoolmaster navigated the warrior's tempestuous temper tantrums and finally earned the man's grudging trust.

After the sea quest, Wiglaff returned to his native village a changed person. He was still the recluse and mystic, but he had a new appreciation for how his unique talents might complement the skills of others in their common objective to defeat the Roman encroachment on Caledonia. Wiglaff felt he was emerging from a seashell into a broader, more mature context than he had ever known. Having traversed Caledonia, he now had a deeper appreciation for what he was protecting. His family was spread straight across the map. All had offered him and his family succor. Together they would face the challenges in the years ahead.

Wiglaff also now saw his sister Winna in a different light. They had worked together on many occasions during which their complementary skills were blended perfectly. They supported each other without envy or bitterness. She had accepted his suggestions. He had understood her need for an active life. She was free in ways he could not understand. He felt he wanted to protect her, but she was fully capable of fending for herself. She knew he would go out of his way to help her, but he never implied she owed him anything for simply being himself.

Through the journey, Mordru gained a new appreciation for his wayward son. It was not admiration. It was more an acknowledgment and acceptance of their fundamental differences, particularly in their divergent qualities of mind. Neither the father nor the son could acknowledge the deep bond that existed between them. So they kept their distance from each other, only connecting occasionally in some common enterprise, usually having to do with Caledonian security.

The tension between father and son was necessary for the lessons Wiglaff would gain from others, particularly from his mentor the shaman. But that may also have been due to Onna's influence. After all, she and the shaman had experienced a love relationship before Mordru made Onna his wife. As the shaman's student, Wiglaff brooded about that relationship until it transformed in unexpected ways and drew his heart as in a maelstrom to depths of feeling he had never known.

Chapter Four

Legacy of Festus

"Slavery in ancient Rome played an important role in society and the economy. Besides manual labor, slaves performed many domestic services, and might be employed at highly skilled jobs and professions. Accountants and physicians were often slaves. Greek slaves in particular might be highly educated. Like modern slavery, slavery in ancient Rome was an abusive and degrading institution where cruelty was commonplace. Unskilled slaves, or those sentenced to slavery as punishment, worked on farms, in mines, and at mills. Their living conditions were brutal, and their lives short."
—https://en.wikipedia.org/wiki/Slavery_in_ancient_Rome

MORDRU, with Wiglaff and Winna accompanying him, observed Roman troops training near their barracks above the wall that had been built during the reign of Emperor Hadrian. The soldiers formed ranks to the north and south of the raised area that had become a shrine for all Caledonians. The ancient Caledonians had once occupied a fort constructed on the plateau. From there they had raided Roman settlements south of the wall until Rome decided to put an end to their belligerence.

Mordru lectured to his children, "On that hill, your ancestors fought until the last man died. Just as the Romans are now ready, the enemy blocked retreat to the north and advanced from the south using means we had never before witnessed."

Wiglaff heard whistling and buzzing in the air. "Father, what are those horrifying sounds I hear?"

Mordru smiled. "You hear death flying in the form of hundreds of metal ingots shaped to make noise as they are propelled by slings employed by ranks of Roman special forces. After the final battle when the Romans retired and left your dead ancestors' bodies to be eaten by foxes and buzzards, your great, great grandmother snuck up on the plateau and collected spent projectiles that littered the ground and stuck in the wooden palisade. Our spies later discovered Rome had experimented with those terrible weapons on us as nowhere else in the empire."

Winna asked, "Was it wise for our people to take a stand where they could be massacred by a superior force from below?"

Mordru, "Daughter, you have hit upon an essential question, answered by our strategy ever since the lessons we learned here. Never isolate your forces on high ground that can be surrounded by the enemy in a siege. Not only do you invite attack by missiles and javelins flung over your battlements, but you also risk running out of supplies necessary for survival."

"Why are the Romans allowing us to watch their exercises?" Wiglaff asked, perplexed, as he nodded towards Roman soldiers who were clearly watching them.

Mordru answered, "They invite us to remember our humiliating defeat. They want us to know they can repeat their sacking whenever they choose to do so. Still, it's wise not to linger. You've seen enough today. We'll withdraw and return to our village now."

Wiglaff wondered about the historical lesson he had learned from witnessing the Roman drills. He also noticed the slaves maintaining the wall and the insignia of the Roman forces doing their exercises. He resolved to ask the freed slave, Festus, why the Romans had not pressed their advantage after achieving their victory. *Surely,* he surmised, *Rome might have marched straight through Caledonia after their victory here.* For some reason beyond his ken, they had not done so.

Winna and her father discussed strategy as they walked back to the village. "Father, how can we expect to defeat the Romans, whose discipline and numbers are so great? They don't advance except in large groups with shields that can lock to form the turtle, impervious to arrows and spears."

Mordru frowned. "Attacking Romans directly will not work for us. Many have died in the attempts to meet them head-on. We've remained free from imperial control because we don't fight anything like our adversary. They expect to win because of massing troops, infinite resupply, and training. Consider how Romans on a field of battle resemble the Caledonians on that plateau you witnessed. Their clear boundaries and lines of dependency give us the advantage as long as we remain distant and relentless, stealthy and smart."

Winna asked a thousand questions about what she had seen. Mordru answered her patiently since he was her mentor in all matters of warfare. Wiglaff overheard what they were saying, but his mind wandered to consider the implications rather than the details. Mordru disdained his son's daydreaming, but he had long given up on making his son into a warrior.

Wiglaff was not jealous that Winna had replaced him, the eldest son, as his father's heir apparent. By remaining separate from the tactical considerations, he could concentrate on strategy. On the one hand, Winna would, at best, become a great warrior like her father. Wiglaff, on the other hand, would become a seer, capable of foreseeing the future for decades or a century.

Arriving at the village, Winna went to help Onna prepare supper. Wiglaff asked Festus to accompany him to his private camp in the forest. They spoke in the Latin language both as practice for Wiglaff and for security. Their conversation, even if overheard, would not be understood by Wiglaff's people, and thus would not have unintended consequences for either party.

"I take it you saw the Roman army training north of the wall today," Festus said, stirring the ground with a stake he always carried. "Now you probably want to talk about the meaning of what you saw." He looked Wiglaff in the eyes and saw he had hit the mark.

Wiglaff approached his question obliquely, saying, "Festus, you're a learned man in Roman terms, but you're not by training or inclination a soldier. You've told me that on many occasions. You've also maintained that Julius Caesar's book The Gallic Wars teaches more than a lifetime's practice in battle. Indulge me a while and tell me why Rome did not press their advantage after besieging our fort to the south of here over two generations ago."

Festus thought for a moment. He looked around the clearing, which was green and peaceful in the afternoon light. "Caesar began the conquest of Britannia, but he had a vision for Rome that encompassed the entire world. His genius for battle might have made his vision a reality, but he was murdered in the Roman Senate. By the time of Emperor Antoninus, the so-called Antoninus Pius, Caesar's dream of worldwide conquest was still alive at the highest levels, but the empire was stretched on all fronts to the breaking point." He paused to let this idea settle in Wiglaff's mind.

Festus continued when the young man nodded. "While the imperial legions pressed at the edges of Caledonia, the Emperor's emissaries were contacting the potentates of the farthest lands of Asia, his merchants were trading with the tribes of India and his generals were plotting war against the Parthians."

Festus drew figures on the ground to represent the geographical boundaries he was discussing. "In the meantime, Antoninus Pius was penurious, not to say stingy. His accountants kept track of his expenditures and reigned in any excess. Instead of pressing his advantage in Caledonia, the Emperor was satisfied he had made his point ... that he could conquer anytime he chose. He stood down and refocused his efforts and resources elsewhere. At the end of his reign, he left a greater legacy in resources than any of his predecessors, but he failed to consolidate his power around the globe."

Wiglaff asked, "And was that a good thing overall? I mean, it was good for Caledonia. But was it wise for Rome?"

Festus smiled and looked at the drawing he had made. "It's always easy to judge from hindsight. When the Emperor's emissaries returned from China, Antoninus was dead. His successor and the recomposed Senate were beset by other priorities after their Parthian battles, including a horrible plague that exhausted the treasury. Some say Rome had passed its apogee." He looked up at Wiglaff gauging his reaction.

"So Festus, what do you think about that view? Has Rome seen its highest point? Will everything now decay and fall to ruin?" Wiglaff asked him.

"Wiglaff, what's important here and now is your opinion, not mine. What do you think?"

Festus's instructional plan was to make his students think through a situation for themselves. Rarely did he intrude on the interior processes of their minds. This made him a great teacher, but many students found the way difficult, even annoying. Wiglaff was not an ordinary student, he embraced the challenges that Festus posed.

Wiglaff said, "My father has reports that Rome is once again massing troops south of the wall. When we rescued you in the north by the sea, it was clear to me that Rome was examining an option for a pincers movement to conquer and enslave our people. Their plan seems to me to be no different from pressing on both sides of our ancient fort to squeeze the life out of the middle."

Festus smiled grimly. "Wiglaff, you're thinking like a Roman. So continue. Tell me what comes next."

Wiglaff knit his brow and looked at the drawing on the ground. "The Roman Senate has decided to provide resources for a great push of historical dimensions. I don't know how this strategy affects the other regions of the empire, but I sense we're going to have to struggle mightily to fend off an attack. This coming fight will determine our future. My father, mother, and sister agree. My aunts and uncles, along with their families also agree. We all know what happened in Britannia ... oppression and slavery. Rome always promises many things to those who capitulate, but it always reneges when it is victorious."

Festus nodded. "Rome considers itself the only civilized force in the world. You Caledonians are barbarians, a nuisance until you can be subjugated. You have no viable choice but to fight. The question is, will your people stick together through many years of strife? Already Rome has been on this great island of Albion two hundred-plus years. Many generations of colonists have been born and died here. Under any worst-case scenario, Rome will prevail at least another two or three centuries at its current boundaries. No other power threatens to overtake it."

Wiglaff squinted at the declining sun. "Still, for over two hundred years Rome has failed to push any farther into Caledonia than their wall with its fortifications. Our raids are little stings, hardly mortal. Rome's only great enemy is Rome itself."

Festus smiled. "What do you conclude?"

Wiglaff shrugged. "I find that we Caledonians must be doing something right. I've had the same dream often of a free Caledonia. The Roman boundaries have been set on our southern borders. For Rome to press northward, it will have to expend a lot of resources, not only to seize land but to withstand a constant insurrection of those who wish to remain free. Caledonians will resist to the last man. I'm sure of that."

Festus nodded and rose. The sun had descended below the tree line. "I'm hungry. Are you going to dinner?"

"No. You've given me much to think about. I'll remain here and think. Please tell my mother that I'll forage for food tonight. She'll understand." Wiglaff had a faraway look in his eyes. Festus knew better than to interrupt his friend's concentration, so he grabbed his staff and departed without another word.

Wiglaff heard the night sounds rise in the forest. Insects and frogs began their mating sounds. The songbirds of the day quieted while the nocturnal birds and creatures ventured forth. Until the darkness fell like a blanket, Wiglaff contemplated the drawing Festus had scrawled on the ground. Caledonia stood against a behemoth that straddled the known world. Yet Rome was testing its limits. Could its limitation of resources dampen its expansion indefinitely? The young man belatedly thought of a hundred new questions he wanted to ask Festus. He brooded while he enumerated the questions in his mind. Playing the part of the schoolmaster, he asked himself the question he knew Festus would ask, "Well, Wiglaff, what do you think?"

Wiglaff's mind wrestled with each question in turn, answering them all with the information he had gleaned. In the middle of the night, he finally fell asleep and continued his thinking in dream visions. He envisioned himself in a cavern on a mountain in a broad plain. All around the mountain, a great battle was being waged for the future of Caledonia. Wiglaff felt vaguely guilty for not being a warrior in the thick of the fray. An ancient voice counseled him to focus on what he saw, not on his guilt and frustration. *"Vision, not foolhardiness, will be victorious."* The young man passed out and slept until dawn.

Festus' school started for Onna's children, but other families heard about his teachings and sent their children too. The former slave was such an excellent instructor that within two years, his pupils were ready to teach the youngest, while they continued their own education. Mordru and the other warriors despised schooling of any kind. They were especially suspicious of the teachings of a former Roman slave who might be a spy. At the same time as Mordru hated the children's progress learning the Latin language of the hated enemy, he had to admit he liked Festus's lessons in basic communication in the Caledonian languages, in which Festus was unusually fluent.

Onna's support of Festus kept Mordru and the other warriors from outright killing him or driving him out of their village. When Festus began to attract students from other areas, he brokered exchanges by which the best of his female students went to teach in exchange for villagers desiring to begin their education. Within four years, Festus's former female students were teaching in villages straight through Caledonia to the northern sea. Festus traveled up and down the region to observe how the instruction was conducted and offer advanced classes on a wide variety of topics.

Through Festus, Onna was able to keep an eye on the villages. She encouraged the schoolmaster to brief Mordru after each of his circuits on the latest news. Among the best news was the fact that the Roman fort far to the north had been temporarily disbanded. The Romans had disassembled the pier they had built and shipped their provisions elsewhere. Forfar reported pillaging the former fort of everything the Romans had abandoned, including the wood from the palisade and weapons the Romans had buried, of which he had sent samples via Festus.

From his pouch, Festus drew heavy projectiles, arrowheads, and spearheads and laid them in a line for Mordru to examine. "Forfar tells me that many more of these weapons lie hidden within the area described for the fort. If you want them, he and his warriors will excavate them and arrange their transport to you."

Mordru picked up each of the weapons and spoke as he examined them. "You have done well, Festus." He turned to Winna and said, "These projectiles are the same kind that we found near the fort where the Roman troops were drilling. They make the whistling, buzzing sounds we heard. We should experiment with them to judge whether we can use them against our enemy. As for these arrowheads and spearheads, take them to Wiglaff for fitting to shafts for our weapons. Their quality is better than anything we've been able to make."

Festus said, "The flints of Britannia and Gaul are superior to anything you'll find in Caledonia. Slaves heat and chip the flints to the sharpness of these heads. As for flinging the projectiles, you'll need to make two forms of slings. Roman special forces from an island in the Mediterranean Sea practice using the slings exclusively. The fact the Romans left these weapons behind means they intend to return someday to reclaim their fort. I wouldn't be surprised to discover that they also buried gold and silver coins under the surface of the fort for future use as well."

Mordru nodded and directed his fierce gaze at Festus. "The next time you go north, have Forfar check the abandoned fort for additional weapons and coins. All weapons he finds should be brought here for our use. Has anything been heard or seen about your companion slaves ... the ones we freed and gave the ship?"

Festus looked around to be sure no one was eavesdropping and nodded. "One slave escaped after the Romans seized their ship and took all the former slaves prisoner. From hiding, Salvius, for that is his name, witnessed the torture and crucifixions of all the rest. Salvius is living with your brother Forfar's family now, helping as a laborer in their fields, a forester in their woods and as a watchman among his warriors."

Mordru seemed concerned. He asked, "What do you think the Romans learned from torturing those men?"

Festus laughed ironically. "They learned nothing they would believe. Torturing slaves in legal proceedings is routine because the courts won't admit in evidence anything uttered by a slave who has not been tortured to elicit it. When an escaped slave has been apprehended, torture and crucifixion are examples for other slaves. A runaway slave is branded on the forehead to denote he was a fugitive. If I'm taken prisoner by Roman soldiers, I'll suffer the same fate as the others. So will Salvius."

"Are you certain that Salvius escaped on his own? I think he might have been allowed to escape to become a spy for the Romans."

Festus thought for a moment. Then he looked Mordru in the eyes and said, "Salvius hates the Romans. Like me, he was enslaved for political reasons. His wife and family were executed, and he was made a galley slave. I talked with him for a long while about his escape. He feels guilty for having abandoned the others. He's also grateful for being alive."

Mordru listened intently to Festus's account. Then he said, "The Caledonian Federation will sort this out soon. In the council, there's been a lot of discussion about the non-Caledonians in the population. The land is riddled with spies, including Picts, and others. The way things are trending now, the others will be the first to die."

Festus nodded. He understood that 'others' included himself. "Should I alert Salvius about this, or not?"

Mordru glowered. "It's best to remain silent. What I've just told you is secret knowledge. Your life would be in danger if you divulged it to others."

Festus collected the weapons and took them to Wiglaff in his clearing. He passed on Mordru's instructions about their use. Under Festus's direction, Wiglaff started right away designing two forms of slings for the projectiles, a long form and a short one.

While they worked on making the slings, Festus mentioned, "Your father Mordru told me about discussions in the council of killing all who were not Picts or Scots in Caledonia. Have you heard any such rumors?"

Wiglaff's eyes widened. "I've heard much about the number of Roman spies in the countryside. Going and coming on our journey to the north, we dealt with known spies in every village. Most of those were Picts. The only two "others" I know about are scattered through the villages, including former slaves like you and deserters from the Roman army."

Festus remarked, "It always starts with a whispering campaign against outsiders. Then the madness spreads like a disease. People naturally fear foreigners and strangers."

Wiglaff said, "I'd be among the outsiders, surely. The trouble is, no one knows where to draw the line between those who can be trusted and those who can't."

"If you hear anything that indicates danger for me, I hope you'll let me know." Festus looked at the sling Wiglaff had fashioned. "That's well done. Let's try it out with a few stones."

Standing at full height and placing a smooth stone in the sling, Festus asked Wiglaff to stand back. He swung the sling at arm's length until it was circling at a great rate of speed. He let the stone fly by releasing one thong of the two-thong instrument, and the stone flew through the air toward the trunk of a huge pine tree. It struck the pine at the height of a man's head. The sound of the collision reverberated. Quickly Festus placed another round stone in the sling and swung it again. As before after he released the stone, it flew directly toward the pine and struck where the last one had.

Winna came running to see what was causing the commotion. She arrived just as Festus was sending the third stone toward the tree. It struck where the other two stones had done and made the same loud wooden sound.

"Hi, Winna," Wiglaff said. "Festus has been trying out the new sling. Three times he hit the pine in exactly the same spot."

Winna nodded excitedly. "Festus, will you sling another stone so I can see?"

Festus shrugged and loaded another one. "Please stand back. Once the sling goes full circle, the force of the stone against the leather can kill a person who gets in the way." Winna backed off and stood next to Wiglaff. Festus released the stone, which flew to the same spot as the former three and hit with the same loud knocking sound.

"Festus, I'd like you to teach me how to use the sling," Winna said. "I believe such a weapon could give us an advantage against the Romans."

Festus smiled. "I've only demonstrated what a simple stone can do as a projectile. If you use a heavier substance instead, it will wreak havoc. And if you fashion your projectile just right, it will make eerie noises as it flies. That way you'll induce fright and tension in your enemy whether it hits your target or not."

He picked up one of the lead projectiles he had fetched from the northern fort and showed it to the brother and sister. "Here's the kind of projectile I'm talking about. This will not only make noise, but it will also lodge itself deeply in whatever it happens to hit. I'll show you."

Festus placed the device in the sling. He made the same arm movement as before and let the projectile fly. This time a whistling sound filled the air immediately and kept sounding until an enormous knock indicated it had struck the pine. Frightened by the sounds, birds rose from the trees all around the clearing. Gesturing to Winna and Wiglaff, Festus proceeded to the tree. On the way, he picked up the four stones that had hit the tree and bounced into the meadow. At the tree, he asked Wiglaff to see where the fifth projectile had struck.

"I found it," he responded. "It's sticking deep in the pine at about the height of a Roman's head." He turned and gauged where the lead would have struck him in the Adam's apple. After all, he was a full head taller than the average Roman. He then used his flint knife to pry the lead object out of the tree.

At the far side of the clearing where Festus had launched the projectile, Mordru and a handful of warriors had gathered on account of the noise generated by the demonstration. Winna ran ahead to tell her father what had happened. As they followed behind her, Festus told Wiglaff how much more advanced the Roman slings-men were over his own humble ability. This was difficult for the young man to believe after the marksmanship he had just witnessed.

Mordru gestured for Festus to demonstrate his abilities to the assembled warriors. Festus obliged. He situated the observers at a safe distance and sent three round stones directly to the targeted spot on the pine tree. This time, he selected a different lead projectile than he had used before. This had two round holes drilled on either side and a ridge raised between them. When Festus released the thong, a buzzing sound followed the object to the pine, where it hit with a loud smack and embedded itself in the wood from which Wiglaff had dug the previous lead piece.

Mordru and Winna shook their heads in amazement. The other warriors were stunned by the prowess of the former slave, whom they had discounted as a mere intellectual and schoolmaster. In a single afternoon demonstration, Festus had acquired the reputation of a skilled warrior. Still, he was not proud. He modestly repeated that he had no special knowledge of the sling. He said he knew much better slings-men, and Caledonians would have to practice hard to be their equals on the battlefield.

Mordru spoke decisively, "Festus, tomorrow morning at daybreak, you'll demonstrate the sling to all our warriors. You and Wiglaff will fashion five slings and find three dozen stones so my men can practice. Once their practice has begun, I want you to travel north again, stopping at each of our family's huts to deliver the slings, and teach their warriors how to use them."

Wiglaff smiled. Now that Festus had made an impression on Mordru, he may have bought immunity from the general fate of those singled out by the Caledonian Federation. Festus proclaimed, "I am an amateur at the sling. Far better than I would be Salvius. Once I have delivered the slings and started the training north, perhaps Salvius can be the teacher in the villages to the north while I govern the exercises for those villages in the south."

Mordru saw the wisdom of this advice and endorsed it instantly. Winna saw an opportunity and asked, "Father, may I accompany Festus on his journey? It would be a learning opportunity for me, and I could provide protection for Festus and refresh our contact with our relatives along the way."

Mordru was not pleased with the thought of Winna's absence, but he approved her plan, more because she could keep an eye on Festus than because she would confirm the family's agenda. He had no fear of Winna's traveling with a former slave for one moon's time. The more he thought about the trip, the more he realized that she would protect a man who, by his proficiency with the sling, was becoming, in his mind, an essential part of Caledonia's military plan. Mordru resolved that he would have Festus introduce the new weapon to the council at his earliest opportunity.

Mordru's plan governed every moment of Wiglaff's existence for the next fortnight. At the end of that period, he and Festus had fashioned two hundred slings. The village children gathered smooth river stones of just the right size to serve as projectiles. Festus planned to take sixteen Roman projectiles to demonstrate the potential for inducing mayhem with the device.

Festus asked for a final meeting with Mordru the evening before he departed on his mission.

"Mordru, thanks for your hospitality. I hope with the sling, I can partially repay your kindness. You should know, though, that among your people lurk many Roman spies. When they discover and report our preparations with the slings, the Romans will not rest until they hunt Salvius and me down and kill us. These projectiles are a Roman state secret, for sharing it … death by crucifixion is the penalty."

Mordru answered, "Fear not, Festus. You enjoy my personal hospitality. Let me ken at the earliest opportunity that you are under threat, and the mighty force of the Caledonian Federation will protect you. In the meantime, count on Winna for your immediate protection. She will guarantee your safe passage."

The next morning when Festus and Winna departed for the north, they carried everything they needed to perform the activities that Mordru wanted. Along the way, Festus taught Winna how to use the sling as well as he did. She introduced innovations that he had not considered. One such was reorienting the plane of circulation of the sling. Another was refactoring the timing for the release of the specially-tooled ingot projectiles to maximize the duration of the eerie sounds they made. Winna devised a way of releasing a projectile high in the air above a force and quickly reloading the sling to send another projectile at the target for effect before the first one hit.

Seeing that he had a warrior genius as his companion, Festus opened up his knowledge of Roman military strategy and tactics, mainly learned from classic books by Julius Caesar and from his own observations as a slave to Roman legionaries. From Festus, Winna learned all about employment of auxiliary forces and earthworks, the Roman practice for orienting forts and devising supply lines, and the use of flanking actions where terrain became a weapon of war. Above all these, Festus discussed with Winna the critical factors that led to victory from the Roman general's point of view: good weather, proper rest, adequate food, the favor of the gods and goddesses and the character of the field commander.

"So, Festus, if the weather is terrible, the Roman legionaries get no sleep and little food, the deities are looking the other way, and the field commander is corrupt and otherwise thought to be unworthy, Rome cannot win."

Festus laughed. "You might think so, but remember Rome thinks it can pick the time and place to fight. Its generals believe they can bribe the gods and goddesses to look favorably on their exploits. As to drunkenness and lechery, no Roman general is immune. Rome depends on its might and mass to overcome all difficulties."

Winna said, "Now I'm confused. Are you saying we should give up and surrender to the inevitable victory of the Romans?"

Festus shook his head. "Absolutely not. I'm just making sure you keep your perspective when you think about your enemy. Look, if you can make Romans strike prematurely, you can throw off their battle rhythm. If you can force the legions to fight while climbing or descending instead of in an open field, they are at a disadvantage. If you can make them think their gods and goddesses have abandoned them, you'll often put them to flight." Festus illustrated his points by waving his hands and sculpting images with his long fingers in the air.

Winna was impressed by the idea that Romans had suffered defeat in battle. She asked, "Can you give me examples of the Romans facing defeat?"

Festus chuckled. "There was the famous case of Caesar Augustus weeping for his lost legions. Yes, from time to time Rome has lost individual battles. Each time, though, Rome came back and eventually won the war. To know Rome, you have to understand the nature of power. Rome's Senate could extend only as far as its budget reached. In considering a conquest, always those who counted the money have looked for the return on Rome's investment in blood and treasure. For example, if trade could be managed without conquest, no army was necessary. If a region was deemed unprofitable or overly complex, the Senate did not want to hear about it. However, if Rome's reputation was at stake, as with Mithridates, it would fund a series of adventures."

Winna said, "Wasn't Mithridates the foe who always came back whenever Rome went home after fighting?"

Festus smiled. "You know your Roman history, Winna. Yes, he was the enemy who always managed to come back to strike again. And you make my point and yours at the same time. Rome can be beaten in battle, but not on the battlefield. There Romans are undefeatable."

For a long time thereafter Winna was lost in thought. She wondered how she was going to defeat an undefeatable foe if all she practiced was her battlefield skills. "So Festus," she inquired, "how do we Caledonians beat the Romans and avoid slavery and destruction?"

Festus thought deeply for a few minutes. "Wiglaff asked the same question, and I'll tell you what I told him. You must combat Rome not with confrontation but with guile. Caledonia must upset Rome's expectations. Consider how—at least thus far—you've managed to force Rome to draw a line, or create a wall that divides civilization from barbarianism. Hadrian's wall is a symbol of defeat, not victory. Likewise, the Antonine wall and the region between the walls. What caused

Rome to stop fighting and erect walls is the secret you're looking for."

In this way, Festus and Winna continued discussing history and strategy as they pressed northward from village to village. At each stop, Winna talked with her family to shore up relationships and discover the news while Festus met the warriors to demonstrate the sling and start the training program for using the new weapon.

At their fourth stop on the way north, they heard unnerving things about a Roman order to stop them, by name. They had to believe what they heard because of the source of the intelligence, a member of Winna's immediate family, her aunt Ewitha, the youngest sister of Onna.

After listening to Ewitha's account, Festus evaluated the threat as a local assassination attempt, by a small group of spies sympathetic to the Roman cause. Winna thought the attack would come shortly after they left the village where they were staying. She guessed their assailants would not know they had been alerted.

Having left the village, they were traversing the hilly country, full of lakes and rivers, when three men appeared directly ahead on their path, evidently waiting for them. Festus and Winna calmly each selected a sling and stone. As they had done in their demonstrations, they let their stones fly. Two of the three would-be assassins fell from powerful blows to their heads. The third rushed toward Festus waving a javelin. Winna drew an arrow and notched it in her bowstring. She aimed and let her target advance to the point where he stopped to launch his weapon. As he raised his spear to throw, she shot him through the neck.

Instead of continuing on the well-beaten path, Festus and Winna blazed a parallel one. They arrived at their next destination a little later than they had planned, but they made no mention of their having encountered and slain the three assassins. The village leader seemed surprised to see them arrive unharmed. He made a fuss about the hardships they must have endured in their travels. He also lamented the absence of three of his villagers, who were still out hunting in the hills. His guests shrugged as if they knew nothing about the mystery.

Festus gathered the village warriors to watch his demonstration. Instead of distributing slings as he had done at all the other villages, the former slave said he would return to equip and train the men on his return journey. Early that morning, he and Winna departed for their next planned visit, careful to watch their rear as they progressed.

"Winna, that village we just left is wholly corrupted by Rome. I suspect we'll see more than three men on their next attempt to kill us. Let's keep alert. I fear they'll likely take an indirect approach this time."

Winna thought for a while as they walked. Her mind was working out the possibilities for their actions. "Tonight, let's start a fire and stand far from it. If someone wants to find us near the fire, we can surprise him with an arrow or a knife. I wish my brother Wiglaff was here to envision what is likely to happen. He's good at prediction … as if he can see the future clearly."

Festus had heard about Wiglaff's clairvoyance. "We'll have to fight without your brother's special insights. Let's keep alert. Above all, we must not be predictable in our actions."

Instead of pitching camp at the summit of a hill, they built their fire just over the summit on the far side. They took positions under an outcrop that gave them shelter from behind. Every hourglass, they put additional wood on the fire and slept in rotation. The five killers came near midnight.

Festus was asleep, and Winna watched with her bow at the ready. She kicked Festus's foot and let one arrow fly into the chest of the largest of their visitors. He fell dead into the fire as Winna's second arrow found another mark. Festus, who had fitted a stone into his sling, now let fly a stone that cracked the skull of an attacker. Two men remained standing, but they were frightened and uncertain what to do. Their confusion made them vulnerable.

Winna shot one man through the arm. Festus cracked another skull with a stone. The only one left alive was the wounded man, screaming on account of his arm. Winna held a knife to the man's throat while Festus interrogated him. Within an hourglass, the assassin gave the names of the conspirators, who included the chief of the village they had just left. Leaving the spy alive was too risky, so Festus dispatched him with a knife run across his throat.

Festus was partial to going forward rather than returning to the village they had left. Winna said, "My father Mordru always counsels to take care of what you know about right now. Delay, and you'll invite compounding of your adversaries and lose the advantage of surprise."

Festus saw the wisdom of that counsel. He cut off the head of the huge man Winna had shot first. Carrying the head by its flaming red hair, he walked back to the village. Winna walked beside him with an arrow notched in case others lay in wait for them.

Festus called for the village chief to show himself. The chief came from his hut with his spear in one hand and a knife in the other. "What is it you want? It's late."

Festus said, "One of your villagers has lost his head." He held the head high. It made a ghastly sight in the low firelight. "Was this perhaps your eldest son, who stood behind you as we passed through your village?"

In the shadows, Winna kept her arrow aimed at the chief's heart. After he decided to rush forward, he took only two steps before her arrow laid him low. The chief's wife emerged, her knife drawn for revenge. She also fell to one of Winna's arrows. Now the villagers all ventured forth and milled around in the square.

"You see that your village chief, his wife, and son are dead. Who among you is now in charge?" Festus asked.

A large man with a full, black beard stepped forward and said, "I suppose I'm in charge. My name is Eadfrith. You've made your point. What do you want?"

Festus replied, "I was given a list of spies for Rome. I want you to arrest these men as I call their names. If you cannot do that … or won't do it, I'll ask my companion to shoot an arrow through your heart. Then I'll ask again who is in charge. We'll continue until I have what I want."

Eadfrith did as he was told. Five men were seized, bound and placed around the fire. Festus began interrogating these prisoners. Each confessed to being a spy. Eadfrith watched as Festus slit their throats with his flint knife. When the last had been slain, the former slave asked the assembled villagers, "Do you know of anyone else who supplies information to the Romans, either in this village or any other?"

Eadfrith shook his head. "You've executed the spies who lived here. Why don't you get along to your next destination and let us bury our dead?"

Winna did not lower her bow. She said, "You'll find bodies of three dead men to the south and five more to the north, one of those headless. We're going to leave now, but mind you, we'll be back. If in our travels we discover that you've lied to us about additional spies, we'll slay both them and you. Do you understand?"

Eadfrith laughed. "Is that the voice of a woman I hear?" He laughed again, but his laughter stopped abruptly as he gripped an arrow that had just pierced his heart.

Festus called out, "Is anyone else laughing?" No one spoke. "I thought not. As the lady said, we're leaving now. Follow us at your peril."

Winna vanished into the night, and Festus followed the path leading to the north out of the village. They passed the five bodies on the hill at dawn. Behind they could see no men following their trail. They stopped to eat, and with Festus standing watch, Winna slept. When she awakened, she watched over him while he slept. By the time the sun was overhead, they continued walking to their next destination.

The schoolmaster and the warrior had no trouble during their next three visits. They demonstrated their weapons, distributed the slings and discussed how the weapons should be trained. Somehow word of their skills had preceded them. They were not challenged though they received some surly looks. In villages where Winna's relatives lived, she gathered intelligence about Roman spies in their midst. By night Festus and Winna sought out and killed those spies, extracting their confessions and the names of other conspirators.

"Festus," she said after a night of ruthless killing, "how many Roman spies do you think infest our land? I had no idea there were so many as we've discovered."

"Romans are patient, and they offer generous rewards, particularly immunity from attack or enslavement after the conquest. Of course, the Romans are lying about their promises. They intend to kill and enslave the entire population of Caledonia. Mark my words … no one will be left free if the Romans prevail." Winna could tell that Festus believed what he was saying. His eyes had a determined look, and he grit his teeth as he thought about the perfidy of Rome.

As they continued north and the rugged land turned into an undulating pattern of hill and dale descending to the sea, they saw approaching Forfar, Winna's uncle. He waved when he saw them and ran up to take Winna in his arms. "I came to find you. A ship full of Roman soldiers has landed. They are camped in the old fort, and have taken Salvius prisoner and intend to brand his forehead and crucify him as an example to other slaves who are tempted to escape."

Festus gripped the thongs of his sling so tightly that his fist turned white. Winna's eyes went wide with apprehension. Forfar understood their shock and pain.

"My warriors are ready to assist you. We have the Romans under surveillance now. I don't know how long Salvius has left. They're torturing him slowly to discover everything they can before they kill him."

Festus asked, "How many Roman soldiers are there?"

"Two guard the ship, which has eight slaves as oarsmen. Ten soldiers are at the fort with Salvius. My men can take the ship and free the slaves, or you two can do that while we free Salvius."

Winna thought about the situation while Festus and Forfar continued to discuss it. "Festus, didn't you say that the Romans were unlikely to believe what a slave told them even under torture?"

"That's correct," he answered.

"As for setting an example by crucifying a slave, is that a good strategy in your judgment?"

"A slave is still a slave in any case … unless he has a real chance at freedom. Fear of crucifixion never affected my actions." Festus shook his head. "But then I'm not your average slave."

Winna nodded and turned to Forfar. "Uncle, how many warriors have you mustered?"

Forfar said, "We are twenty strong, myself included."

"How often do the men in the fort communicate with those by the ship?" Winna asked.

"They've been coming to relieve the watch at noon, each day," her uncle answered. "Four come, and two remain replacing the watch of two, who walk back to the fort as a formation of four."

Winna said, "Festus if something were to happen to the four on their way to the ship, what do you suppose would happen?"

Festus thought for a moment. Then he said, "The two guarding the ship would become worried. They could not leave the ship because the Roman standing orders mandate having at least two men guarding the ship and its slaves at all times."

"And what would the soldiers at the fort do when the four men did not return in the evening?" Winna asked him.

Festus nodded because he saw the young woman's logic. "They would likely send another four men to see what had happened to the first four."

Winna said, "By my count, that would leave two soldiers guarding Salvius. Is that correct?"

Festus nodded. "Yes, it would. Are you thinking what I'm thinking?"

Forfar interjected, "My men can kill the first four and the second four coming from the fort."

"Meanwhile, I can kill the two guarding the ship and free the slaves," Festus said. "I'll know soon enough whether the slaves want to be freed."

Winna said, "That leaves me to kill the two soldiers left at the fort and to free Salvius. We'll have to hurry to set up. Does anyone have questions?"

Forfar ran to rally his troops to set an ambush for the four Roman soldiers along the path from the fort to the shoreline. Festus ran ahead to the vicinity of the ship. With his sling, he sent two missiles against the heads of the two Roman soldiers who were standing guard. He had no trouble after that freeing the slaves. He quickly identified the slave most likely to be an informer. Without remorse, he slew the man with his knife. He ordered the other slaves to row their ship away and enjoy their freedom.

Winna watched the first four Romans leave the fort. She trusted her Uncle Forfar to kill them all. Four hours later, the second group of four soldiers left the fort. Winna expected her uncle would kill those as well. She saw one soldier standing on a high platform scanning the area. One of her arrows pierced his neck, and he fell silently. She ran to the open area where the palisade once wrapped around the fort. In the center of the area, the remaining Roman soldier was engrossed in torturing Salvius, who was still alive. A cross had been erected nearby for his crucifixion. The slave had been cruelly branded on the forehead. The branding iron lay red hot in the fire.

Winna shot the soldier in the back of the head, so her arrowhead pierced his brain. She cut Salvius free and gave him water from a nearby container. The man could barely walk, so she held him up until he had the chance to get the circulation back in his legs.

A commotion made her leave Salvius standing while she wheeled and notched an arrow in her bow. She saw two Roman soldiers fleeing a line of pursuing warriors. They were running for the fort, screaming for assistance. Coolly, Winna walked up the steps to the platform overlooking the area. She aimed and shot the nearest fleeing Roman soldier. Her uncle, heartened, flung his spear into the back of the last surviving Roman.

Forfar and Winna knew what must come next. They helped their warriors burn the dead so that they could not be found. In the process, they collected the soldiers' weapons and provisions. Festus joined them to relate what had happened with the Roman ship.

"The slaves have already rowed well out to sea heading south along the shore. They are free, and the spy among them has been killed and buried alongside the two guards' corpses." Festus continued, "Before they departed, one of the slaves told me the ship had been sent all the way from the other side of Caledonia to kill us if we made it this far. News seems to travel fast. I must conclude that the Romans are worried about our strategy with the slings."

Forfar smiled and said, "All the more reason to get right to the demonstrations and training. We'll feast tonight. Tomorrow at dawn, we'll begin our training."

Hobbling and bloody from torture, Salvius said, "Count me in! I'm hurt, but at least I'm not hanging on that cross." He gestured toward the cross intended for his crucifixion. He laughed long and hard. "Thank you for saving my life, but I'm hungry. What can I eat?"

Festus shared dried meat with Salvius and helped him down the path to the village. That night a bonfire was the celebration for overcoming the Romans and freeing the slaves and Salvius. Venison and rabbits were roasted. They ate bread that had been baked in Roman figure-eight ovens. Forfar broke out mead, made from honey, and they drank liberally.

Festus helped Forfar's wife dress Salvius's wounds. They applied ointments and used linen bandages. Winna observed their ministrations since she was trying to learn as much about treating battle wounds as possible in a small amount of time.

The next morning, the demonstrations and training went as planned. Festus distributed slings and stones to Forfar's warriors, and a drill regimen was established. Festus observed as the warriors took their first attempts at using the sling. He gave pointers and, occasionally, did secondary demonstrations all day long.

At the evening meal around the communal fire, he told Winna, "We've completed our mission. Congratulations to us! We have established a program of using slings as weapons all along the path from the wall to the sea. It's up to the villages to perfect their use of these tools. What do you think about all that we've done?"

"Festus, we couldn't have done this without your expertise and skill. What bothers me is the speed and accuracy of Roman communication. Before we were halfway through the villages, we had spies and assassins dogging our every step. The ship waiting here when we arrived must have moved like lightning to be in place before we arrived. I'm still trying to think through why the Romans captured and tortured Salvius. Will you please explain to me how they did it?"

Festus hesitated before he replied. "Romans could not have communicated as speedily as they did without their spies among the Caledonians. I don't mean one-time informers. I mean spies embedded in the villages, reporting frequently, perhaps even daily. The Romans must have known I was involved. Salvius was taken because he knew me. They thought I might come to rescue him. In fact, though, you did that part. I only freed the slaves and encouraged them to take their ship and flee."

Winna thought about this. Then she asked, "Do you think the Romans will discover what happened here?"

"Even if they don't learn all the details, they'll guess what happened. They'll also be back. As you may recall, I predicted that they would return. They are creatures of habit. Once a fort has been established, it serves as a magnet. They shall return."

Forfar, who had overheard their conversation, said, "Each time we deal with the Romans here, we are practicing for the time when we'll have to stop their attempt to provide a blocking action against our retreat from the south. As long as my warriors and I can stop them, Mordru will only have one front to fight, not two. The Romans are formidable. We only managed to kill six of eight before the two last soldiers fled for the fort. We lost no men because we stood at a distance under cover and used our javelins. We had plenty of spares, and they only had what they carried. Many warriors threw wide or short. We'll have to practice our aim more diligently than before. I understand you two are leaving at first light tomorrow. Do you want an escort for your journey?"

Festus looked at Winna with a smile and asked, "What do you think?"

She looked into the fire with her flashing eyes. "I think we'll manage, Uncle Forfar. Thanks for your hospitality. You did the right thing to wait until we could join forces before you attacked the Romans. The way we attacked held the lowest risk. We were lucky to get to Salvius in time to save him."

The next morning, a low mist covered the landscape as Festus and Winna started walking south. The path was rugged and steep rising from the shore. They startled entire deer families feeding and drinking from the streams. As the sun rose and burned off the mist, they enjoyed the view. Gorse and bracken gave way to copses of trees and, in the distance, forests rising above the hills. The path was familiar now, and the villagers expected them, eager to show what they had learned.

Now Winna asked penetrating questions about Roman spies. She learned that some suspects had fled, fearing discovery. A few troublemakers were told to leave or keep quiet. Winna's frown showed she meant business. Her uncles and aunts were briefed by Festus and herself about how to spot a spy and what to do when they found one.

Festus did not give away all his slings. He kept a short one and two long ones, with projectiles just in case of further trouble. Winna still had plenty of arrows in her quiver, and she carried extra bowstrings. Occasionally, she shot and dressed a deer for food. In each case, she ate the raw heart and liver for energy. Festus learned to drink the blood of a freshly killed animal. The carcasses and hides of her kills were appropriate gifts to their family members in the villages as they walked south.

Festus and Winna's walk from village to village, with stops to eat and sleep, had taken two full moons venturing from their home village north of Hadrian's Wall to the northern tip of Caledonia.

***

Wiglaff welcomed them at the edge of the village when they returned home. He told them, "You will need to report right away to Mordru. He's been waiting impatiently for your return. Much has happened in your absence, but he'll fill you in." As they left to find Mordru, Wiglaff retreated to the clearing in the forest where he had been collecting feathers and spores.

Winna knew her brother's habits. "Festus, don't be bothered by Wiglaff's preoccupation. He's in one of his meditative moods. As for me, I feel at loose ends because our mission's over. I've finished one, but I crave taking on another right away, but I know reporting to my father is our first priority."

Festus said, "I understand how you feel, but I have the advantage of being a slave. I go along with what my masters tell me. I don't complain. I've won too many stripes with a whip to think differently."

When they found Mordru, he pushed his daughter aside and drew Festus close to him to hear the news.

Winna was naturally disappointed when Mordru had asked Festus, not her, to report what happened. She brooded about it and thought, *After all, the mission was his, not mine. I was only Festus' security.*

Winna later learned that her job, by Festus's account to Mordru, was performed to perfection. Still, she felt neglected. That evening while Festus was regaling her father with stories, Winna snuck into the forest to be with her brother. She found him lost in a trance before the dying embers of a fire. She put another armful of kindling and a log on the fire for him. Before long, the fire was casting long shadows, spitting and crackling.

Winna sat on one side of the fire while her brother sat on the other. They both looked at the fire, not at each other. Winna wondered what her brother was thinking. What had he done while she was protecting Festus? She tried to put herself in his place but failed. After a while, she fell asleep, exhausted by her long excursion.

Winna awakened at the crack of dawn. She saw Wiglaff looking at her across the embers of the fire. He was smiling. "So you came to watch the fire, and I was in a trance?"

She nodded sadly.

"I take it Festus made his report to our father?" Wiglaff asked, guessing the reason for her disappointment.

She nodded again. "It was Festus's mission, after all. I was just along to help and watch his back. I did that, to be sure. Our father took it for granted that I would bring Festus back alive."

"Why should he have thought otherwise?" Wiglaff asked with a smile.

She shrugged. "It wasn't easy."

He shrugged. "It never is. Yet here you are. I'm glad you're back. I had troubling dreams while you were gone. I saw you kill eight spies one night, three at once, and then five more. I saw you kill two Roman soldiers in a fort. Then you killed a third running toward you. I was afraid for you, but I knew you weren't afraid though I wondered how you manage not to be."

"Not to be what?" Winna asked.

"Afraid."

"How do you see so clearly what's happening when you're so far away?" Her eyes were squinting, examining his face for any slight change in his expression.

Wiglaff cocked his head, but he did not answer. His eyes got a faraway look. He said, "I'm afraid of what's coming for all of us."

"What ... with all the spies?"

"It's the Romans, and the spies are part of that." Wiglaff was tempted to describe his visions, but he withheld his expression of them. He was still wrestling with the details he recalled, and then he had to work out their meanings.

He said, "The shaman is coming soon, and I'll be working with him closely. You and I won't have the time to talk or be together as we are now. It will be as if I'm on a long journey, but, don't worry, I won't be far away."

Winna replied, "It will just be like you're in a trance, I know. A long one. Only you'll finally be with someone who can share your visions for a change." She smiled ruefully. She still felt excluded from his secret world of spirits.

"I suppose you're right. How are you getting along with Festus?" Now Wiglaff had an impish expression and an insinuating smile.

Winna turned her head from side to side and looked at the ground. "I think he's all right. I mean, he's excellent with a sling. I wouldn't have thought so until I saw him in action."

Wiglaff nodded. "Is he better at being a schoolteacher or at being a slings-man?"

"Either way, he's a good man first. Fortune played a cruel trick to make him a slave for a while. I can't get rid of the image of Salvius being tortured next to a cross erected for his crucifixion."

Wiglaff nodded. "I saw that vision too. I think it must have been through your eyes. I saw the letters branded on his forehead. I watched you dressing his wounds in Uncle Forfar's hut. Our aunt was there. Festus was there too. You were weeping."

Winna blinked. "Yes, I think I was, but please don't tell anyone. Oh, Wiglaff, how do you know these things?"

The future shaman closed his eyes and said, "Our father is looking for you now. He wants to know why you planned the action around the Roman fort as you did. Festus could not tell him the reasons for your judgments. Mordru suspects you may have many secrets to tell him about your trip. For now, you should go." He opened his eyes and looked at her so earnestly, she had the strongest desire to weep. "Warrior women don't weep," she told herself.

She stood and shook her limbs. "I must be going, Wiglaff. You'll stay right here?"

He nodded. "I'll be right here." His eyes were focusing on a flight of birds in the morning sky. When he looked around to see her, she had gone.

Chapter Five

Shaman and Mentor

"A shaman heals both the living and the deceased. In healing those who died, the shaman performs a psychopomp ceremony of helping those who have died cross over to a comfortable and peaceful place. The ceremony may also include clearing a home or land of spirits that are in a state of unrest. A depossession might need to be performed to clear a person of unwanted spirits."
—Sandra Ingerman, http://www.shamanicteachers.com

AFTER lunch one day, Onna sought out Wiglaff in the clearing in the forest where he dwelled. As she found him meditating, she sat down opposite him and waited for him to emerge from his trance-like state. She had no idea how long he had been lost in his dream world. Likewise, she had no idea when he was likely to re-enter the world of other mortals. Deciding that she would wait only until the sun fell below the treetops, Onna breathed deeply. Feeling confident that Festus could handle the small children with his afternoon lessons, she leaned back and enjoyed the spring day.

In the distance, Onna heard the faraway sounds of military training exercises. Mordru was exercising his noisy male warriors. Winna was drilling her women warriors with less fanfare. In the meadow before her, she watched the purposeful flights of colorful birds and the random paths of insects. The news she bore was both sad for her and happy for her eldest son. Ugard, the shaman, had sent a messenger to fetch Wiglaff to begin his training.

***

If Wiglaff departed, his mother knew he would be changed as he applied the rigorous regimen of shamanism. She wondered whether the young man's character would necessarily change. The training had not changed Ugard's character. Not even his long trip to Rome had affected his friendly relationship with her. On alternate days she felt relieved that the time had come for Wiglaff to seek his destiny outside the village. Still, she counted on him. If anything happened to Mordru, Wiglaff as his eldest son would inherit leadership of his family even though he choose to be a shaman.

Wiglaff's stern father, the paragon of warriors, had first suggested, in anger, that his son leave the village to become a shaman. "The boy is useless as a warrior. Always daydreaming and skulking off to be alone, he's a disgrace to my name and our family. The sooner he leaves, the better." That was what Mordru said as he stomped off to lead one of his raids upon the Romans.

Yet Onna knew her son's intelligence and insightfulness far better than her husband ever did. She was not sure that the shaman's way was right for Wiglaff. At times, she was outright negative about the idea. Why did Wiglaff have to choose a path? He was doing just fine being himself. She counseled her son to bide his time and depart only when he was sure the shamanistic path was right for him. Meanwhile, she took the initiative to contact Ugard suggesting he consider making the boy his apprentice.

Onna reflected on Ugard. She and Ugard had been close and might have married if Mordru had not proposed marriage first and hustled the young woman into matrimony. Ugard had been hurt by Onna's decision at the time. Because of her marriage to Mordru, the shaman left the village and went abroad to Rome to study for over twelve years. Onna missed talking with Ugard, but she had a growing family to raise and might have feared Mordru's jealousy. When Ugard returned from Rome, he took up residence in a huge cavern on the mountainside near the village. Occasionally he dropped by Onna's hut when Mordru was off fighting to check on the progress of Onna and her children. She could tell by the way he looked at her that he had never lost his deep feelings for her, but he never acted inappropriately. They were just good friends.

Ugard told Onna during his first meeting after he had returned from Rome, "When you were betrothed, I vowed never to interfere in your family life. Crushed as I was by your choice to marry Mordru, I was freed to follow my destiny as a shaman. I don't regret what fate has decreed. I hope you have no regrets. Anyway … we are what we are."

Onna, who could always speak openly to her friend, asked, "As a shaman, did you find what you were looking for in Rome?" She was trying to do four different things at the same time: herding two toddlers, changing a baby, shucking peas and cooking dinner. Ugard was amazed at how effortlessly she managed to do all the right things as she shifted back and forth among her tasks. He liked the way she unselfconsciously scooped her long hair behind her ears to keep it out of her face.

He answered, "Onna, Rome is reputed to be the center of the world. I found it the center of all the evil in the world. I was lucky to escape and luckier to have a cavern to inhabit on my return here. In Rome, I learned things I could never have mastered at home. I studied with the most talented magicians of both white and black magic. What I encountered will serve me well in my role as shaman. I have no desire to take another such journey. I'll live out my life on the mountainside until I retire. Will you tell me how Wiglaff is doing? Do I discern in him the fatal signs of budding shamanistic skills?"

Onna shook her head. She had been expecting this question with dread. She started from a basic fact they both understood. "Well, you can imagine his father's disappointment. The boy will never become a warrior. He's a dreamer and a thinker, just as you were before you departed. He's the opposite of everything Mordru stands for." She paused with a glance at Winna, who was listening to her conversation.

Onna gestured for Ugard to follow her outside. "Winna, please watch the children for a moment." Outside the entry, a deer carcass was aging on a raised stake in the ground. She cut strips of venison with her flint knife while she continued her train of thought. She offered some to Ugard, but he demurred. She shrugged and continued her work, saying, "Winna is Wiglaff's opposite. If she weren't a young woman, her father would make her one of his warriors. She has all but taken the boy's place in her father's affections."

"So, Onna, what are your plans for Wiglaff if he isn't going to become a warrior?" Ugard seemed genuinely concerned, and he saw from Onna's averted eyes that he had hit a tender nerve. "I'm sorry to be prying, but the question is important."

She looked at her friend's expression and saw genuine concern. She said, "Not to worry, Ugard. Wiglaff's future consumes many of my daytime hours. He's done many things that few warriors could accomplish. He makes weapons better than anyone else ... even Mordru grudgingly acknowledges that. Wiglaff's mind is strategic. He's always thinking about the answers to why things are happening and what would be required to remedy difficult situations. His father can only think of tactics. Mordru doesn't have the patience for contemplation. Wiglaff is never rushed, but his judgments are sound. The depth of his insights is unique in our family. Do you know what I mean?"

Ugard looked at the ground. "Wiglaff is a born strategian. His quality of mind requires time and quiet. Does he have to choose a profession right away?"

Onna nodded, her brow knit in worry. "Mordru's impatience is the reason. I'm not sure how much longer he'll tolerate Wiglaff's continuing his private path. As you know, conflict is continual among the villages, the clans, and families. Things are heating up. Men are dying every day. I'm worried that Mordru will force Wiglaff into arms and get him killed."

Ugard looked around the village square. Women and children were peacefully getting ready for dinner before their men returned. They were doing the things that mattered most in life. They performed the everyday tasks that made huts into homes. "If ever you need to get Wiglaff out of the village — providing he feels the urge to study the arts of becoming a shaman — I stand ready to accept him as my apprentice. Don't answer me now. Just keep my offer in mind. I know it's unfair and inappropriate, but I think of your children as the family I never had. I'd like to help."

"Thank you, Ugard. I know how difficult it is for you to make this offer. Your privacy and isolation have always been important to you. Your calling always made me sense I was on the outside of a secret world I would never understand. I won't pressure Wiglaff, but if he asks for an opportunity to grow by being a shaman, I'll remember your kind offer. Again, thank you. Now I'm going to have to hurry to get ready for Mordru's return. Drop by the hut whenever you like, but preferably when Mordru is away. It's good to see you again after all these years. It almost seems like yesterday when you went away. I thought I'd never see you again. That made me very sad."

That first visit by Ugard was the first of many, but the subject of Wiglaff's education never came up again in their many conversations. Onna saw Ugard carefully observing Wiglaff when he dropped by unexpectedly. The shaman occasionally brought gifts of rare feathers, unusual rocks and hides of small animals, like mice. Wiglaff looked forward to Ugard's appearances before he became the woodland recluse on a permanent basis. Mordru was only one reason for Wiglaff's self-imposed isolation. Another reason was the difficulty posed by the crowding in Mordru's hut. Wiglaff's dreaming only worked for him when he was not constantly bombarded by having to deal with others. Boys and girls of his age in the village did not understand him any more than their parents did. If he had not left the village, he would have been cast out, ostracized or even killed outright.

Onna observed the situation without commenting upon it. When the village wars started, and the chaos of fighting became dangerous for everyone on a daily basis, Onna knew it was time for her family to go north to stay with relatives and for Wiglaff to go to Ugard's cavern to study.

Wiglaff told his mother, "I don't think I can avoid involvement in the village fighting much longer. Maybe if I prove myself in battle, my father's view of me would change. What do you think?"

Onna responded, "You'd only get killed. You're not warrior material. Recall how many men have died, and they spent each day training. You may be brave and strong, but those traits are only the beginning. Unless you're willing to put every ounce of your being into fighting, you'll eventually be slaughtered. In fact, if you live by the sword, you'll die by it. Mark my words."

Wiglaff thought about this warning for a while. Then he said, "You're right. So what am I to do? Maybe it's time for me to see Ugard the shaman and get his opinion. He's always seemed to understand what I am. What do you think?"

Onna sent a messenger that very afternoon to Ugard. Her message was simple: "It's time for Wiglaff to begin his training with you. Let me know if that is all right with you. If it is, I'll send him to you straightaway." Ugard responded affirmatively and immediately by the same messenger: "I couldn't be happier. I'll expect his arrival day by day."

***

Onna watched the butterflies and dragonflies as they flew through the air above the clearing. When her eyes returned to Wiglaff, he was looking at her and smiling.

"You've come out of your trance," she said with a smile.

He nodded. "Yes, I have. Thank you for not interrupting me. You've come to tell me Ugard will accept me as his student. The answer is that I'm to leave at once. Is that all right?"

Onna's eyes widened with surprise that her son had somehow divined her purpose in being there in the clearing. She seldom visited him in his quiet space. She remarked, "I don't know how you know these things, Wiglaff. The messenger only just arrived at the village with the news this morning. Are you happy?"

"I'd say the news comes just in time. In another day or so, I'd have been drawn into the fighting by my father. I'll pack my things and go to the mountainside tonight." He sprang to his feet and pulled his things together. Onna handed him a pouch full of seeds and dried berries. She kissed him on the cheek, and he grabbed her in an enormous hug and held her. She wept at the thought of his absence.

When he let her go and backed off, she said, "Soon, I'll have to take the children north along the path. We'll remain there until the worst of the fighting is over. Winna will protect us on our journey. Right now, you should think of nothing but your training. I know your becoming a shaman will be good for you and the whole village someday. Be safe. I'll look forward to seeing you upon your return."

Wiglaff departed wearing and carrying the hides that were his clothing and shelter. In his left hand, he carried the bag of food his mother had given him. In his right hand, he carried a bag with his small collection of feathers, stones and animal bones. By sundown, he was making his way up the mountainside to the cavern where Ugard dwelled.

Outside the opening to the cave, he saw a torch in a makeshift sconce. He used the torch when he entered the cave to find Ugard meditating on a bearskin. Rather than disturbing his future mentor, Wiglaff laid the bag of food on the corner of Ugard's bearskin. He spread his own skins on the floor in an empty corner of the cave and fell fast asleep on top of them.

The next morning, Wiglaff was awakened by the deep sound of someone thumping a pigskin drum. Outside the entrance to the cavern, he saw Ugard beating the drum with a wooden club and chanting. The shaman had braided feathers in his hair. He wore only a rabbit skin garment around his waist. Wiglaff could see the shaman's body was lean and muscular. He watched the shaman perform his ritual for at least one hourglass.

When Ugard finished pounding the drum, he entered the cave and, without a word to Wiglaff, opened the bag of food and offered some to his apprentice before he partook of it himself. "Why are you here?" Ugard asked him.

Wiglaff answered, "I'm here to learn how to be a shaman like you."

Ugard squinted and said, "You'll never be a shaman like me, no matter how hard you try." He said this matter-of-factly. Then he sat on his bearskin rug and began meditating in the same posture that he had assumed the night before.

Wiglaff imitated him in every outward way as he sat on his own bearskin. He was determined to prove he could be a shaman exactly like Ugard. This was the beginning of the first phase of Wiglaff's training when he desperately mimicked his mentor in every way.

From sunup to sundown and then all night long, Wiglaff did what Ugard did. The shaman paid him no attention. Ugard provided nothing by way of tools, so Wiglaff had to make everything he needed by himself. For example, he studied Ugard's pigskin drum until he understood how it was made. He then killed a boar, skinned it and dried the skin. He built a wooden frame over which to stretch and tie the hide, which he soaked so it would shrink to fit as a drum cover. He also found a piece of wood that he shaped into a drumstick. The next time Ugard beat his drum at dawn, Wiglaff stood beside him making the same sound and chanting low as his mentor did, wearing only a cloth made of rabbit skin around his waist.

Ugard descended from the mountain three days in seven to disrobe and immerse himself in an icy stream where he chanted and ducked under the surface in a pattern Wiglaff imitated. When their bath ended, the men spread their arms and looked directly at the sun as their bodies dried. As the weeks went on, their bodies became increasingly alike, both skinny and muscular. Ugard needed little food to stay fit.

Wiglaff ate no more than his mentor. When Ugard ate mice and rats, Wiglaff fashioned wattle baskets to harvest rodents. He watched how Ugard sacrificed the animals, removing their pelts and drying them for various purposes. With flint knives, the shaman and his apprentice removed the skins and then ate the vertebrae, heart, and liver of each mouse, rat or vole. The remaining meat they dried before their fire.

A moon had moved through all its phases before either man spoke a word to the other. The first to speak was Ugard as he came out of a trance at midday. "Did you, Wiglaff, know a man named Festus?"

"Yes, master, I did," Wiglaff answered. "He was a former Roman slave who is protected by my family. Why do you ask?"

Ugard nodded but did not speak. Instead, he went into a trance, Wiglaff did the same and tried to envision Festus but could not do so. He heard Ugard's voice whispering, "Do not force the vision. Let it come of its own accord."

Wiglaff relaxed and breathed deeply, then exhaled. He thought he was falling asleep when he saw an image of Festus fighting a throng with his sling. Arrows were hitting attackers as well as stones from his sling. Wiglaff sensed that Winna was fighting alongside the former slave, but he could not see her. Festus fought heroically, but the numbers of the assailants were too great. He was taken prisoner and carried off.

Wiglaff came out of his trance, but Ugard was still meditating. Wiglaff tried to interpret what he had seen. He remembered his mother warning about the increasing violence among the villages. For a moment he feared for his family because Festus was to accompany them when they fled to the north. He resolved to ask Ugard what the vision meant.

Ugard remained in meditation the rest of the day and well into the night. Wiglaff began meditating while he waited for Ugard to come out of his trance. Once again he saw Festus, only this time the former slave had the brand mark on his forehead. He was being tortured and interrogated by four Roman soldiers, but he refused to say anything no matter how intense the pain. Frustrated, the soldiers raised Festus's body on a cross at the center of the raised fort just north of the Wall. He hung there bleeding while guards paced back and forth below. Finally, he died, and Wiglaff awakened.

It was dawn, and Ugard was pounding his pigskin drum outside the entrance to the cavern. Wiglaff jumped up to join the shaman with his drum. He entered a trance just as Ugard had done. In that state, he did not see the mist rising from the forests or the sunshine cutting through the scattered clouds. Instead, he saw Festus's body being taken down from the cross. A small group carried the body past Roman soldiers with arrows sticking from their dead bodies. Festus's body was taken to the village square. Mordru appeared and pressed his warriors, but Wiglaff could not hear what his father was saying. When he awakened, Wiglaff was still pounding on his drum, as was Ugard.

Wiglaff felt hungry, but he was not going to stop beating his drum or chanting. Quickly, he slipped into envisioning again. He saw that Festus's body was being buried with full military honors as if he had been one of his father's warriors. Beside the grave stood twenty clansmen, one of whom was the image of Festus himself. When the body had been covered with earth and overlaid with small stones, the twenty departed, but the image of Festus remained contemplating the grave. Wiglaff felt uneasy about this vision. Festus turned and looked him directly in the eyes. The ex-schoolteacher mouthed the Latin word 'fugitivus' and smiled horribly. Wiglaff came out of his trance to find himself alone. He stopped pounding his drum and went inside the cavern where Ugard was eating seeds and dried berries.

Wiglaff did not talk about his visions. He ate what Ugard ate and thought about what he had seen and experienced. He learned a few things that answered some of his questions. He learned that the first vision was answered by the second, and the second by the third. He knew in his heart that Festus was dead. The man had been killed by the Romans. His dead body had been retrieved by his father Mordru and his warriors then buried near the village. Something about the spirit of Festus remained alive even after the body was buried. Questions remained about why Festus had been fighting and about the fate of Onna, Winna and the children.

Wiglaff decided to meditate to discover the answers to his new questions. He wondered whether he could approach the spirit of Festus for the answers. He noticed that Ugard had already gone into a meditative trance. Therefore, he wasted no time. Wiglaff meditated and soon after he drew his third deep breath, encountered the spirit of Festus.

"Wiglaff, is that you?" Festus asked.

Wiglaff said, "Yes, I am Wiglaff. Are you Festus, the former slave?"

Festus said, "I was that man when I remained among the living. Now I'm lost and don't know what to do. Will you help me?"

Wiglaff was in an entirely new realm. This was the first communication with a spirit he had ever experienced. He tried to remain calm. "Tell me how you feel."

The figure of Festus raised his arms and did a pirouette before jumping into the air. "I feel no weight. I have no sense of urgency. I feel drained and lost. I'm disappointed because I can no longer be of service … to anyone. I'd say I want to return to my body, but that way has been closed to me. Even if it weren't shut off as a possibility, I still have memories of excruciating pain. But where will I go next? I'm of a mind to stay right where I am because that's easy to do. I'm not sure that's the right thing to do because I feel a great injustice has been done to me. I'd like to take revenge."

Wiglaff said, "If I could help you arrive at the Elysian Fields, would you go with me?"

Festus thought about this for a very long time. Finally, he said, "I think I'd like that very much. Yes, I'd go with you. When do we start?"

Wiglaff felt his body relax. He breathed out slowly until he thought he had expired. Like the flickering of a flame, he envisioned ears of autumn wheat and oats. He extended his hand, and Festus grasped it. Suddenly, the figure of Festus was standing waist-high in a field of grain, and an unnatural sunshine shone over the vast landscape. The sky was the brightest blue, and a gentle wind blew over the tops of the grain, making the field undulate like waves in the sea. A seraphic smile spread over Festus's face, and he released Wiglaff's hand. At that moment, Wiglaff felt cold water on his head, and he gasped.

The worried face of Ugard looked down at him. He dipped a cloth into cold water and squeezed it on Wiglaff's forehead. "I thought you'd died for a moment. Cold water did the trick. Breathe deeply now. Continue in a gentle rhythm until I see you've got your color back."

Wiglaff smiled faintly. He twitched his fingers and toes and realized he could sense his extremities. After a moment, he sat up. He had the strongest impulse to pick up his drum and beat it outside the cavern. He looked at Ugard with wild eyes. The shaman nodded as if he understood from experience what Wiglaff had been through.

Wiglaff drank from the bowl of water that Ugard held. He then stood up and grabbed his drum, taking his position at the mouth of the cavern, he began to beat the drum as he went into a trance. From far off he saw a figure in a field of grain that extended across the horizon. He then saw his mother Onna and sister Winna playing with the children. He had a warm feeling that his family was safe somewhere in the north. He saw his father Mordru slaying warriors and smiling while he did so. Wiglaff was glad to see his father in his element. Gradually, Wiglaff's drumbeats quieted. He stopped and went back to his bearskin where he collapsed for the night.

The next day at dawn Ugard went to immerse himself in the icy stream. Wiglaff did the same. They both drank from it, and Wiglaff ate the watercress that crowded the bend. He also tickled a large trout and cast it on the bank for breakfast. A group of six warriors laughed at the shaman and his apprentice when they emerged naked from the stream to dry themselves in the sun. Ugard and Wiglaff paid them no attention. They continued with their routine, eating the trout for breakfast when they returned to the cavern.

As they ate their fish, Ugard remarked, "You've accomplished your first psychopomp." His tone was approving, but Wiglaff was confused.

"What's a psychopomp, master?"

"What do you think it is? Think about what you've been doing and tell me." Ugard's eyes now appraised his apprentice with a look that implied that Wiglaff had everything he needed to respond.

Swallowing before he began, Wiglaff told the shaman what he had envisioned. He focused primarily on Festus's spirit. He explained about the spirit's desire to be transported to Elysium. "The spirit said he felt lost and did not know what to do next. I suggested he might want to go to the Elysian

Fields. When he liked the idea, I fell into a deeper trance and when I saw the Fields, held out my hand and fetched him there. He smiled when he saw where I had taken him. Then he released my hand. I came out of my trance feeling the cold water you were dropping on my face."

Ugard pursed his lips. "I was afraid you had died, and I was not far from being right."

Wiglaff said, "I'll try to interpret what you just said." When Ugard nodded, he continued, "When I reached the Elysian Fields, I was in a death like state, something like the spirit had attained. If he had not released my hand, I might have remained where I took him. Just as I was the medium to take him where he needed to go, you were the medium to bring me back to the world we see around us."

Ugard nodded, reflectively. "Go on, my son."

Wiglaff at first did not know what to say. Then he gritted his teeth and said, "I had the strongest feeling I should not leave the spirit of Festus in our village. It had told me it felt lonely and wanted retribution. It knew it could not go back inside the body of Festus. Harm might have been done by the spirit. So by taking the spirit where it needed to go, I not only was able to heal it from its own feelings, but I was also able to heal our village from any harm the spirit might cause it."

Ugard said, "Exactly. In this case, you had the advantage of knowing the person before his spirit was released from his body. You also were lucky that your father and his warriors were able to retrieve the body before his spirit departed from it. You haven't told me everything you envisioned, though. Do you care to proceed?"

Wiglaff blinked. "Oh, yes. I also saw that my mother, Winna, and the children are safe and that my father is also safe and happy fighting against his foes."

Ugard stood and walked to the mouth of the cavern. He put two fingers in his mouth and whistled, the sound carrying over the forest. He extended his arm and waited for a long time. Wiglaff saw an enormous winged figure come out of the pitch black of the night and land on Ugard's arm. It was a large barn owl. Ugard transferred the bird to a wooden perch he had fashioned near the back of the cavern. He then opened one of his wattle cages and extracted a large, white mouse. The owl hooted and nudged its head toward the shaman. Ugard gave the owl the mouse. When the owl took the mouse in its beak, Ugard held up his arm. The own hopped onto his arm. Ugard carried the owl to the entrance to the cavern and let it fly into the night.

Wiglaff watched this sequence and wondered what it meant. He was going to ask about that, but Ugard anticipated his question and said, "While you were working on Festus, I was trying to resolve a number of spiritual issues at a village close to the Roman camp just above the Wall. Dealing with spirits—of both Caledonians and Romans—is somewhat tricky, especially when you start with distrust all around. Now that you've cut your teeth with Festus, perhaps you'll want to go to the next level and try to heal a village?"

Wiglaff nodded. He was exhausted from his first lesson. He resolved to get some rest before he went to the second level of shamanism. As he had received no coaching to achieve what he did with Festus, and assumed he would receive no coaching as he explored the next level either. He was right, of course, as shamanism must be learned from the inside rather than from the outside and by personal experience rather than rote memory. The young man now knew from his experience that he had the insights within him. He had no idea how he was going to discover how his visionary powers fit together to form solutions.

The next morning Wiglaff went down to the stream alone to bathe and feast on watercress. He had left Ugard at the entrance to the cavern beating his pigskin drum. The shaman-in-training was beginning to understand why Ugard had told him he would never be like his mentor. Imitation alone was not the magical key to shamanism. Wiglaff now knew he had to proceed alone in parallel with his master while Ugard still was evolving in his trade. The shaman's techniques did not put Wiglaff off or make him feel slighted. They did not lead him to disrespect his master. Instead, they affirmed something he had known from the earliest stages of his consciousness.

Wiglaff entered the water and sank beneath the watercress, so only his head remained above the stream. Over the water came the sounds of warriors on the move from both sides, converging on the stream. The rival warriors fought a bloody, vicious battle. Many fell dead near and in the water. The battle continued, but the field shifted from the stream to the nearby forest. Wiglaff emerged from the water and allowed the sun to dry his hair and skin. He put on his loincloth of rabbit skins and collected the weapons of the fallen warriors. He carried the armload of weapons up the mountainside and deposited them in his corner in back of his bearskin.

As Ugard was sleeping deeply, Wiglaff decided to discover the current state of the combat among the villages. He went into a trance and envisioned each of the villages, from the village that lay just north of the Wall to his own village, one by one. He did not envision the situation north of his own village though the troubling visions of the others suggested that he would find similarities all the way north to the sea.

The first pattern Wiglaff discerned was that villages, including his own, were fighting against all adjacent villages in an apparent free-for-all with each one fighting for itself alone against all others. All villages were on a war footing daily. Any aged people, women and children were at constant risk of being slaughtered. The shaman-in-training witnessed bodies piled high in burnt or burning villages, fields stripped of harvests and animals and warriors wandering through the landscape killing everyone unable to defend themselves.

The second pattern he discovered was the increasing number of Roman scouts throughout the area. Roman military intelligence was keenly interested in the civil war that was growing in Caledonia. The scouts made contact with their spies in the villages, who stoked the fires of ancient wrongs and insults into open conflict. External incitation was clearly a major factor keeping the village wars going to weaken Caledonia in preparation for the Roman invasion yet to come.

The third pattern he found was disconcerting. Of all the clans and families, his own had been most provident, moving the women and children north before the conflict became so intense that finally, no one could escape. Among the strongest competing groups of warriors were those led by Mordru and a man named Gilthu. Those factions avoided conflict with each other while they attacked any of the other groups with impunity.

Wiglaff emerged from his trance in a cold sweat, panting from fright. He saw Ugard watching over him while feeding a crow, perching on his arm, strips of rabbit. The young man's flesh crawled at the idea of carrion birds eating dead meat as the crow was doing. All the villages he envisioned were haunted by flocks of black birds, from vultures to crows, devouring human entrails and putrefying flesh. Ugard's crow eyed Wiglaff and cawed mercilessly as if it could read his mind. Wiglaff told his mentor what he had seen and the three patterns he had divined.

Ugard nodded and said, "What you've envisioned thus far, Wiglaff, is only the surface of what's going on." Ugard smiled grimly. "When you've had time to rest and eat, meditate on what lies underneath."

Wiglaff ate and drank sparsely so that excess would not spoil his envisioning powers. While he was recuperating, Ugard released his crow, which flew out of the cavern and over the forest. The shaman then sat on his bearskin and entered a trance of his own. Wiglaff watched his role model look inward. His breath became faint. His skin tone became pale. The man held his thumbs against the second fingers of each hand, turned up on his knees. Ugard's back was straight. Wiglaff's posture was similar, but he preferred to lean forward slightly and roll his eyes upward.

As his mind expanded to consider the abstractions that lay beneath the surface of the village wars, he stopped himself from forcing conclusions. He allowed the spirits to come to him. They did not disappoint him. The first to appear was the image of his great-great-grandmother, who had gathered projectiles from the old Caledonian fort that had been besieged.

"Woe betide those who forget the terror of the Roman siege," she wailed. Her withered hand reached out to touch Wiglaff's face. Her bony hand felt cold and clammy. He envisioned through that spirit's touch the siege itself, the projectiles cast from slings whistling and buzzing through the air, impacting everything and killing the humans they touched either immediately or eventually since they were coated with poisons. Some Caledonians tried to escape from the fort to the north, but the Roman soldiers stationed on that side sliced them to pieces. Even those who fell on their knees to beg for mercy met instant death.

Wiglaff asked the woman, "What can be done to avoid the ruin ahead?"

She smiled a deathly smile. "Eventually, all will die. The question is whether they will die as slaves or as free men and women. The spirits of the Caledonian dead are a form of hidden army, but they don't have a way to channel their wrath to affect the Romans. Will you be that channel for our wrath? I don't think so. You are not a warrior. You're a shaman-in-training." She laughed out loud.

"Are you truly the spirit of my ancestor?" Wiglaff asked her. "Or are you a wicked impostor, emanating from the Roman dead to deceive and mortify me?" This stopped the spirit for a moment. Wiglaff watched her transform into a Centurion's shade.

The Roman soldier's shade gave Wiglaff a sneer and then vanished. Wiglaff continued to envision wondering what other false images would appear in his mind. He saw a chariot advancing on a plain followed by legions advancing at a run, in blocks with shields and spears. In the chariot rode the Centurion, who intended to put Wiglaff to flight. The shaman-in-training stood his ground as the whole spirit army passed through and around his insubstantial form.

Next came a horde of former Roman emperors, from Julius Caesar through all those who succeeded him. They posed as all-powerful monarchs, prideful and haughty. They said with a single voice, "Bow before us since we are Emperor gods."

Wiglaff was not intimidated. He told the shades, "Return to Hades where you belong. You've tried conquest and failed. Give up and seek elsewhere to shore up your idea of global domination. Caledonia shall remain free even if we have to fight to the last man, woman, and child. We shall resist. Count on that and despair."

The shades of the emperors vanished like smoke. Then a beautiful Roman priestess came through the smoke. She was stately and poised. She wore a white gown. On her heels, she wore golden wings. Instead of insults, she bowed slightly before Wiglaff and caressed his face with her hand. Her eyes searched his, their four pupils wide with wonder. Wiglaff extended his hand, which passed straight through her image. She smiled and said, "We'll meet again, and you shall become my father."

Wiglaff came out of his trance, shaking his head. Of all the four visions, hers was the strongest and strangest. Was she an indication of his final defeat? That's not the feeling he got from their encounter. What did she mean that he would become the maiden's father? As he drank and ate, he kept the girl's image in his mind.

When Ugard came out of his trance, he saw that Wiglaff had changed. "Will you tell me what you envisioned? Tell me everything, at once."

Wiglaff then recounted what he had seen in detail. He told about the deceitful spirit who had taken the form of his great-great grandmother. Then he described the Centurion and his army. He went on to discuss the long line of emperors from Julius Caesar forward. "Their spirits," he said, "tried to intimidate. I stood firm against them. I believe I succeeded."

Ugard said, "There's more, isn't there?"

Wiglaff nodded. "Yes, there was a girl, a priestess in a pure white robe. She wore golden wings on her heels. Her touch was warm. Her eyes were gentle. She said I would become her father."

Ugard's thumb and fingers stroked his chin. His eyes looked down. "She's a surprise. What do you make of her?"

Wiglaff thought for a moment. Then he fixed his eyes on his mentor's. "She was the only spirit who came from the future. Funny how she's the only Roman spirit I actually feared."

Ugard stood and gestured for Wiglaff to step outside the cavern with him. They stood side by side overlooking the forest in the night. Bats flew by them chasing insects. The crescent moon shone on the treetops. "Your visions have been focused in the past and the present. I'd like you to be open to the future now. The appearance of the girl indicates you might be very good at that. You won't have to force yourself. Just don't block the future from presenting itself to you. Watch the heavens where I point my finger."

Wiglaff watched as Ugard pointed. At first, he saw nothing. As he accustomed his vision to the night sky, he first saw stars. Then he noticed that everywhere Ugard pointed, a shooting star appeared, but not beforehand. He said, "Ugard, are you making the shooting stars appear where you're pointing?"

The shaman kept pointing without speaking. The shooting stars kept appearing. The more Wiglaff watched the demonstration, the more he was convinced that Ugard knew in advance where the shooting stars would appear. When the demonstration was over, the shaman went to sleep on his bearskin. Wiglaff stayed awake all night thinking.

The shaman-in-training understood his master's nocturnal lesson as being about foreseeing the future. How much of the future could a shaman like Ugard actually see? Was it possible he could envision ahead decades or even centuries? Clearly, he could foresee what was going to happen in the heavens. Or did he cause the heavenly events to occur by orchestration? If that were true, what might that power mean for orchestrating other events?

***

Wiglaff thought back to his first weeks of study with the shaman. He had, he thought, come a long way since then. Now every day he was learning something new. More than that, he was learning about the power that lay within himself. When the crescent moon fell below the tree line, the young man stepped out to watch the night. He pointed his finger at a random patch of sky. No shooting star appeared where he pointed, but with averted vision, he saw a shooting star appear elsewhere. He played a game to guess where the next shooting star would appear. After pointing several dozen times without success, he shrugged.

"For now, the shaman has a talent I cannot fathom. I won't be anxious to learn how to predict the motions of the heavens. What good could that kind of prediction cause anyway? I shall try to remain open to the future presenting itself to me. If the Roman girl is an indication, I have a natural start in that direction."

The more Wiglaff dwelled on his powers, the more he discovered how much he still had to learn. For example, he knew a lot more about the motions of the heavens than he admitted to himself. He knew about the movement of the sun and the moon. He also knew how the stars swept through the heavens in the night. Obvious celestial motions were comforting to him. Shooting stars were anomalous and seemingly random. They did not have a logic like the phases of the moon.

Likewise, aside from the changes of the seasons, the weather seemed to have fewer patterns than anomalies from his point of view. He struggled to predict the next day's weather, but he was not good at that just yet. Rain was his forte. He could do well in predicting rain. Ugard praised his knowledge of rain. "That will save a shaman's life in planting season," he said. "Of all predictions, rain is most important.

Keep practicing with rain. That has utility beyond all the celestial phenomena. You'll see. Soon enough, you'll see."

Wiglaff became adept at observing shamans elsewhere. He thought about his envisioning shamans as an extension of his learning. In addition to Ugard, he envisioned shamans in other villages. He did not like what he saw. Some shamans were slovenly and slack. Others were charlatans. As he observed one deceiver try to bring rain, he watched the man's villagers hack him apart with their knives and axes. Another shaman was a lecher who lured young girls into his lair and despoiled them. He was discovered and slain by an outraged father. Wiglaff saw that the other shamans had little to teach him. Ugard was a shaman of a different order from the others. That insight ended his focus on the practices of other shamans. He looked first to Ugard and, more and more, to his own, innate abilities.

Unerringly, Wiglaff could predict rain. He could never articulate why his predictions were precise. The more he studied himself, the more he became convinced that the relation between his shamanistic powers and the rain was innate. When he asked Ugard about this, the shaman told him, "I'll teach you the ritual of bringing the spring rain. Then you'll know the truth. Rain can be predicted … you demonstrate that repeatedly. Now you're going to have to focus on bringing the rain even when your predictions indicate no rain will fall."

Wiglaff was bewildered by Ugard's logic. "If a shaman can cause the rain to fall by performing a ritual, why does his predictive power have any meaning at all?"

Ugard smiled and shook his head. "You'll see," he said. "But you'll have to puzzle out the reason for yourself."

The ritual of the rain was complicated. Once Ugard started teaching this critical ritual, he would not allow Wiglaff to think of anything else. For a complete moon cycle, Wiglaff only watched Ugard make all preparations for bringing the rain. He learned about the implements, the feathers, the grains and the stones used in the ceremony. He also learned how to define the area for divination, within which the shaman would stand and sit while he performed the ritual. More than that, he learned the manner by which the villagers were to participate in the ceremony.

Ugard said in a stern voice, "Rainmaking is a supremely communal effort. No shaman working alone can bring the rain in a way satisfactory to complement the spring planting. Remember that thought each year when you perform the ritual to bring the rain. If you forget it, the villagers will instinctively know they have been cheated. The bonds between them, the shaman and the spirits will be broken. The only remedy for them is to kill the shaman and replace him with another."

Once Wiglaff had witnessed every aspect of the preparation advised by Ugard, the shaman allowed him to help do the preparations again from the beginning. This time Wiglaff had to find all the ingredients for the ritual by himself. Another two moons passed before the preparations were complete. Ugard felt that Wiglaff was, finally, ready to witness the ritual of the rain as the shaman performed it in a village. He did not select Wiglaff's community for the demonstration. The risks of combat were too great, and the villagers had not properly prepared the fields. Instead, Ugard took Wiglaff to a village well north of the current fighting.

The shaman of that chosen village had been hacked to death by the villagers. Therefore, Ugard explained to Wiglaff, "Two things have to be done in quick succession. First, we must heal the village. Second, we must bring the rain. I'm going to prepare for the ritual in the village square while you heal the village by contacting the spirit of the deceased shaman and lead him away from the village."

Wiglaff was terrified about executing his task. He had no idea what Ugard meant by leading the shaman's spirit away from the village. Having no choice, Wiglaff could not complain without violating the mentor-apprentice bond. If Ugard ordered him to divert the spirit, he would do so by whatever means possible.

Ugard inscribed the square with the geometry necessary for the ritual. Meanwhile, Wiglaff spread his bearskin on the ground outside the shaman's former dwelling and went into a trance. A band of children gathered to watch the stranger meditate. Wiglaff ignored them even when they climbed onto his bearskin and touched him to see if they could disturb him.

Wiglaff had no trouble locating the disgruntled spirit of the murdered shaman. The spirit confessed, "I will plague this village with all manner of misfortune. I deeply resent your presence. I plan to interfere with the rain ritual and cause your shaman to be hacked to death just as I was."

Wiglaff knew he had to act fast. He told the spirit, "I can help you ruin the ceremony, but you'll have to come with me to fetch the new grain to substitute for the grain he'll use for the ceremony."

The spirit liked this idea. He gladly took Wiglaff's extended hand while the shaman-in-training went into a deep trance to reach the Elysian Fields. There, he revealed the golden grain rippling in the sunlight. "I'm going to release your hand for a moment. You gather as much grain as you can in both your arms. When you're ready, we'll return to the village to do harm."

The spirit released Wiglaff's hand and jumped into the field, pulling up sheaves by the handful and tucking them in his arms. The more grain the spirit picked, the more he wanted to harvest. He became lost in his own activity. Meanwhile, Wiglaff backed away and left the spirit behind.

Ugard was almost ready to perform the rain ritual when Wiglaff came out of his trance. The shaman looked at Wiglaff significantly, and the shaman-in-training nodded that the spirit had been removed. The villagers were now all assembled as Ugard said they would be. Wiglaff quickly rolled up his bearskin and went into the hut of the former shaman. He did not want to interfere with his master's ceremony, but he watched everything from inside the hut.

Ugard performed the ritual exactly as he had described it to Wiglaff. In rapid succession, the clouds came, the thunder and lightning followed, and then came the rain, which filled the irrigation ditches and left the village and its villagers soaking wet, yet infinitely grateful. Ugard walked over to the hut where Wiglaff was waiting and told him to follow him out of the village. The two men walked through the muddy square and continued walking back toward their mountainside. The village chieftain ran out to thank them for performing the miracle and to offer them a hut where they could stay indefinitely. Ugard shook his head slightly indicating he did not want the offer, and the chieftain went back to his village.

Ugard told Wiglaff, "He'll have to find another shaman. I make it a practice never to remain long where a shaman has been killed by the villagers. They get in the habit of killing their shaman, and there's no end to the killing. By the way, how did you deflect the spirit of the shaman they hacked to pieces?"

Wiglaff smiled ruefully, "I led him to the Elysian Fields and left him there happily harvesting the golden grain in the sunshine."

Ugard cocked his head and regarded his apprentice with new respect. "I would never have thought of doing that." From the shaman's droll expression, Wiglaff could not tell whether he was joking. As if reading his mind, Ugard said, "I don't joke about things like that. When I said, 'I would never have thought of doing that,' believe me. One day, perhaps, you'll show me the Elysian Fields. When that happens, of course, I'll want to come back with you to the land of the living."

After that exchange, the mentor and apprentice continued their journey home to the cavern and spread their bearskins on the earthen floor for their nightly meditations. Wiglaff was glad to have experienced the ritual of the rain. He was also pleased to have been successful in diverting the butchered shaman. As he drifted off to sleep, Wiglaff wondered seriously whether he would find the shaman's spirit waiting for him the next time he ferried a spirit to the Elysian Fields. The thought of the betrayed spirit standing in the field with his arms full of grain made him shudder. Then he shook his head, smiled and slept until morning.

CHAPTER SIX

The Calling

"Spirit calls us to a path of shamanism in many ways. It can be as dramatic as a life threatening illness or as simple as a dream. Some people receive signs of a shamanic calling through their dreams. Shamans frequently journey during their dreams, often flying through the air. Shamans may have recurring dreams in which they meet certain animal or teacher figures that are manifestations of the very spirits who are calling them."

–http://shamanicdrumming.blogspot.com/2013/08/signs-of-shamanic-calling.html

WIGLAFF began his day by accompanying Ugard to the stream for their full-immersion bath. In the water, the shaman began intoning a rhythmic chant, and Wiglaff followed the disjointed melody. Ugard suddenly stopped chanting, but his apprentice continued, lost in the song. When they were drying in the sun afterward, the shaman asked a question that took Wiglaff aback.

The shaman asked, "Do you have a true calling to be a shaman, Wiglaff? Or are you just going through the motions? I know you have the gifts. You've demonstrated what you can do naturally often enough. You also have the stamina and determination. What I'm worried about is something that does not come from you exclusively."

Wiglaff replied, "Master, I'm not sure what you mean by the phrase 'a true calling.' I've always felt I was different from the others. By nature, I'm a recluse. I have clairvoyant powers that I used before I came to study with you. My mother told me I was born to be a shaman. My father mocked me by saying the same thing. Will you tell me how you received your calling? Maybe that way I'll know whether I've received the same calling too."

Ugard ignored Wiglaff's question. Wiglaff shrugged and pulled on his rabbit-skin loin cloth. He resolved to examine his past life for any indications of a calling. He was confused and wondered whether Ugard was looking for an excuse to disown him as an apprentice and possible replacement. For the first time since he arrived, Wiglaff had serious doubts about why he was here. Given that the villages were at war, he wondered whether his choice was dictated more by circumstances and less by a deep commitment to the shamanistic ideals.

Wiglaff went back to basics. He meditated on his entire life, as much as he could recall of it. His superior memory allowed him to relive each moment of his past as if it were occurring at that moment of reflection. He recalled the first time he encountered a poisonous spider. Others in his family were instantly repelled, but he edged the creature from its corner in the hut onto a leaf. He carried it far into the forest and released it in a rotten log. Onna had been thankful to be rid of the pest, but Wiglaff wondered at the time why he had been bold and not terrified.

He carried the themes of the poisonous spider through his life. Each time a dangerous element was introduced into his life, he thought through the implications coldly and acted to remove the threat. *Is this form of problem-solving akin to the shaman's role?* After long contemplation, he thought not. Similar events involving a poisonous viper, a rabid raccoon, and a vicious boar came to mind. In each case, his grace under pressure allowed him to deal with the situation when all others were afraid.

Wiglaff switched his frame of reference to human interactions. His father had always been the most admirable and terrifying influence in his life. His disapproval of Wiglaff from his earliest memories was absolute and unaffected by anything Wiglaff did. Even when Wiglaff's intelligence sorted out the crux of a situation, Mordru degraded his inputs as merely intellectual, not physical. His father's military mind thought in terms only of combat against a clearly identified threat. Mordru liked the clarity of orders from above. Wiglaff hated being told what to do when the direction was not going to be productive from his perspective.

Wiglaff's tendency toward being alone was encouraged by the disapproval of all grown-up villagers. It was also underscored by the hatred the other children had for him. No one understood why he liked to be alone. They would not accept his views even though they hardly had the patience to listen to his explanations for them. His skills as a listener and spy were legendary among the villagers. He was a natural detective. He could see through deceit in a minute. Wiglaff could find something when everyone else had given it up for lost. He could also vanish when he seemed to be in plain view and remain hidden so no one but his sister Winna could find him.

He reasoned that his distrust of humans and their suspicions about him were not essential to the question Ugard had asked. He began to think about his instances of clairvoyance. Here again, his powers of envisioning were unparalleled in his village. He had an uncanny knack of knowing what was happening even when he was not present to observe the events himself. No one had asked him to see what he saw. Visions had come to him in dreams and daydreams. *Is this the unbidden power that my mentor wants me to realize is my calling?* He thought not, as others had dreams as vivid as his own. Many had foreseen things just as he had. The difference was Wiglaff knew what he saw was true. He never had a doubt about the accuracy of his visions.

Now Wiglaff felt he was on the right track, reasoning at a higher level of thought than he had ever done before. The breakthrough was not in the practical manifestations of his visions. Rather it was in his inner conviction about what his visions meant. As he reviewed his visions through his life until this moment, the pattern of conviction was clear. Just as clear was the pattern of those visions coming to him of their own accord. Confident that he had a firm foundation for meditation, he went into a trance to continue his thoughts in his inner mind, without the external interference of the senses. For him, it was as if his eyeballs had turned inward to see not visible manifestations but invisible forces of the mind and spirit.

What made him capable of leading the spirit of Festus to the Elysian Fields? Wiglaff was not a Roman. His only previous thoughts about the fabled Elysian Fields was taken from verbal accounts of Festus himself. He had no prior idea of what he would do to conduct a spirit to the realm he had never seen or foreseen … a realm that may not even exist. Yet under pressure to relieve Festus's spirit of its anguish, Wiglaff had known exactly what to do. He had taken the spirit by the hand to the Elysian Fields and released the hand once the spirit realized it was finally home. Ugard had called his service psychopomp, and that word gave to his mission a firm reality that linked to his later service in the village that had killed its shaman.

Why had he known exactly what to do when Ugard left him to deal with the lost and vengeful spirit of the butchered shaman? Wiglaff had no specific instruction to do anything but divert the spirit any way possible. So the apprentice had done what he knew how to do only by experience. The shaman spirit had no knowledge of the Elysian Fields. Yet Wiglaff had escorted the spirit to that realm and left him there. More interesting was that he had returned to the land of the living without the dire effects that he had after his first visit to Elysium. Did that mean he was now becoming accustomed to conducting a psychopomp? Either way, the spirit had been diverted. The shaman had told Wiglaff he was surprised at the young man's solution. Did that mean his innovation was wrong in the shaman tradition? He did not think so. He had been ordered by Ugard to solve a problem, and he had done so, making up his actions out of whole cloth as he went. He mused that he had done what his sister Winna always did … acted before all the details had been thoroughly considered. Hadn't he always advised her to plan before she impulsively acted? Why was the same tactic so attractive to him?

In his meditation, Wiglaff then wondered too about his visions of false spirits, whose intent was to trick or deceive him. The false ancestor spirit, the Centurion figure and the long line of Caesars came to him unbidden. Were they part of a false calling? Or was there something of a calling in his ability to see through their lies to the truth and to spurn their advances? Despite these questions, the would-be shaman was convinced his sifting and winnowing truth in the spirit world was a special ingredient of his calling.

Thinking about the maiden in the white toga with the golden wings on her heels, he was thrown into doubts of a different kind. He had been physically attracted to the maiden. When he thought of her now, his heart beat faster. He longed to see her materialize again. Yet she was clearly in Roman clothing. She was a priestess. And she was from the future. Was his clear view into the future an indication of his calling as a shaman? He felt he should not jump to that conclusion because that future had not happened. He decided to exclude all future visions except for those which could be verified by history. That much, he thought, was fair. While Ugard had encouraged him to practice envisioning the future, the question of his calling needed constraints. Otherwise, he would be adding upon delicate matters. Wiglaff wondered whether such decisions to exclude were signs of his calling.

Wiglaff ended his afternoon meditations no further ahead. He came out of his trance to discover Ugard feeding a white mouse to a hawk perched on his arm. The gigantic bird flew out of the cavern and made a direct flight to a tall oak tree where its nest lay. Ugard saw his apprentice's frustration and offered him a bowl of dried fruits and seeds.

"Do you want to talk about what you've seen so far?" Ugard asked. "I won't try to influence your thought patterns. It might, however, help you to explain what you're casting about in your mind."

Wiglaff took a deep breath and exhaled. He did not look his mentor in the eyes as he said, "My role as a psychopomp is clear to me now, and I understand that I can see the future clearly. I've been meditating on visions that came to me spontaneously, but those are complex and two-sided. I've had false visions come to me as well as true, and in my trance, I know the difference." He now looked up and found his mentor's eyes fixed on him. Ugard nodded.

"I've reviewed every event and every envisioning of my entire life until this morning. I've realized the answer to the question of my calling is at a level of thought above the visual. I'm going to try envisioning without a clear reference to see what turns up. After I get some water, I'll begin."

Ugard remained silent while Wiglaff drank and repositioned himself on his bearskin. When his apprentice had entered his dream vision state, Ugard began his own meditation on his separate bearskin. A light rain pattered on the landing outside the cavern. The afternoon outside had become a pervasive, melancholy gray.

Wiglaff gave no direction to his wandering mind. After emptying it of all conscious content, he let it drift at will. His eyeballs raised up under his eyelids, and his mind's eye trained on his soul. His body twitched slightly as if his spirit wanted to escape. Suddenly his spirit was flying over the world, eyeing the landscape as if it were a high, swift-flying bird. It flew over his village where attackers were being repulsed by a warrior Wiglaff knew was Mordru. It then flew south to the Roman Wall where the soldiers were marching in rigid formation. It flew farther south and saw a great fleet at anchor and warehouses full of provisions. A massive gray creature with a long nose was being used as a beast of burden. Hundreds of slaves were carrying things in all directions. Overseers were directing the activities. Women were being conveyed in guarded litters. An orator was declaiming on a dais while men in togas listened to his every word.

Wiglaff's spirit flew back to the north along the path through the villages to the sea. He saw Caledonians going through their evening routines. Early fires were being started, and roasting stakes were being driven into the ground. The would-be shaman's spirit continued all the way to the coast where Forfar's village lay. The Roman fort area was empty though a Roman ship had pulled onshore. Romans and Caledonians were locked in combat. Wiglaff recognized his uncle and the former slave named Salvius, both using their javelins and knives while fighting at close quarters. When the Roman leader tried to thrust his javelin at Forfar, Salvius threw his body between the men and took the thrust intended for his uncle. This gave Wiglaff's uncle the opportunity to slay the Roman leader, but Salvius was dead.

As Wiglaff hovered to see what would come next, Salvius's spirit rose to greet him. The spirit asked, "Wiglaff, is that you hovering over the battlefield?"

"Yes, Salvius. I'm grateful for your having saved my uncle from the spear. I'm sorry for your loss. You will be missed."

"Will you take me where you took the spirit of Festus?"

Wiglaff extended his hand, and Salvius took it. The shaman-in-training saw that the spirit's visage no longer carried the brand mark. His brow was spotless now though his eyes lacked the luster of the living. Wiglaff fell deeper into his meditation and found the Elysian Fields. There he released Salvius's spirit in the golden field of waving grain. In the distance, he saw a figure that might have been Festus. Wiglaff withdrew quickly now that his job was done. Again his spirit hovered over his uncle's village. The Romans were not to be seen. The villagers were placing the last stones on Salvius's grave. Forfar looked into the sky right at Wiglaff, but by then Wiglaff was heading south again. Too fast for flight, Wiglaff was back in the cavern, emerging from his trance, sweat gathering on his brow and dripping down his arms. He saw that evening had fallen. The cavern was lit with torchlight. Ugard was meditating on his bearskin. Wiglaff smiled and, after eating a handful of seeds and dried berries, he took a long drink at the basin that caught the rain water. Afterward, he fell into a profound sleep.

That night Wiglaff dreamed of the Elysian Fields where his spirit had taken the spirit of Salvius. In the dream, he saw the spirits of those two men, each standing alone like statues in the perpetual golden light. In the distance, he saw the spirit of the butchered shaman, who mouthed something Wiglaff could not hear. He drew near to the shaman and heard, "I never dreamed of this place, yet you knew of it and brought me here. I should be wrathful at your betrayal, but I'm grateful and at peace. What shamanistic powers do you wield to do what you do? I never knew the like."

Wiglaff was not inclined to answer the spirit's question. The spirit became preoccupied and froze in place. Wiglaff then found himself in a mountain setting, wandering among the crags and peaks effortlessly until he reached the summit of the highest mountain. From that vantage, he could see the edges of the world. He had never seen this vision before, but he knew he saw on his left the triangle island of Albion. He saw in a patch of sea the boot that must be Italia. Far off to the right, he saw the expanse of Asia and an ocean looming beyond where the sun rose over islands in the distance. He was amazed at how much water lay spread out as rivers, seas, and lakes. At his elbow stood the young girl in the white robe. She seemed to be enjoying the view as much as he. He felt an impulse to speak to the beautiful vision, but she raised two fingers to her lips for silence. Then she was gone, and he was in the cavern again on his bearskin listening to the patter of raindrops. In the torchlight, he saw that Ugard the shaman was fast asleep, his hand holding an amulet made of a dun red stone.

Ugard and Wiglaff did not converse except for essentials during the next moon. Ugard wanted Wiglaff to brood on his calling. Wiglaff genuinely wanted to sort the matter out for himself. To that end, he was entirely absorbed in his personal meditations. The village wars might not be happening except for the sight of occasional fires of huts burning in distant villages.

Winter came with a heavy snow that blanketed the landscape and made the paths up the mountainside impassable. Ugard and Wiglaff had prepared for the season in advance. They did not require much for sustenance, but they had laid in plenty of dried meat, seeds, nuts, dried berries, and fruits. They melted snow for water and bathing. Some nights they slept out on the landing so new snow covered them entirely.

Wiglaff struggled with his visions and his internal questions. His quest had become redirected by considering the girl in the robe and her statement about his becoming her father. He could not fathom why she had said that. He thought he must know the reason before his quest was over. He never mentioned her to Ugard in the moons since their last conversation, but the old shaman knew what his apprentice was thinking. One particularly clear winter morning, he decided to break the impasse in his student's thinking.

After he had taken a drink of melted snow, Ugard asked, "What about the girl in white troubles you, Wiglaff?"

Wiglaff's eyes grew wide with surprise, but he realized his mentor had unique gifts too. He shrugged. "I'm supposed to become her father. I can't figure out how that can happen."

Ugard said, "There's no reason a shaman cannot marry and sire a daughter."

Wiglaff nodded. "She did not say she was my daughter. She told me she would become my daughter."

The shaman shrugged, "Adoption is an option. In Rome, it happens routinely, even at the imperial level. Caesar Augustus was adopted, for example."

"I suppose she could eventually be my daughter-in-law and not my natural daughter," Wiglaff ventured. Then he added, "Also, she appears dressed in the garb of a priestess."

"Are you troubled you might marry, and your wife might bear a son?" Ugard asked, smiling at the idea.

Wiglaff took no offense at his mentor's amusement, but he said in a stern voice, "I have no time for personal relationships now. I've got to master my trade."

"Still, you're troubled enough to have been sidetracked from considering your calling to think of this spirit. Could you be suppressing an instinct to find a girl and marry her?"

Wiglaff flinched as if he had just suffered a blow. "I don't think so. It's true that I'm physically attracted to the girl in white. She's unlike any woman I've ever known."

"So are your mother, Onna and your sister, Winna," Ugard observed dryly.

"They're different. They're family. This girl is dressed like a Roman. I can't figure out what that might mean. You've been to Rome; can you help me sort it out?"

Ugard breathed out and in. He looked out over the forest where the black branches were hung with sparkling ice and snow. "Rome is full of beautiful women, the like of which you've never known. Still, Onna outshone the brightest among them. Having known her as a youth, none of the others could tempt me. As for you, I know of no woman who has captured your heart. One day a woman may do that … and you should embrace the opportunity for a wife and family."

Wiglaff nodded. "What do you make of the golden wings she wears on her heels?"

Ugard said, "Those are the symbols for the Roman god Mercury. The image you've conjured is a priestess of that god. Beyond that, I don't know what to tell you. You're on your own. I can say that your vision is about the future. No one is sure about how our relationship with Rome will evolve."

"Yet you've been to Rome and walked among the Romans. You've learned their language and discussed religion with their priests and priestesses. More than that, you've studied with the greatest magicians of our time. And you came back here to live a reclusive life as a shaman."

"All that you say is true. What's your point?" Ugard asked a little snappishly to return his pupil to his quest.

Wiglaff looked out at the sun shining on the forest. "My point is that I'm as much involved with Rome as with my visions. When I was in my meditations a while ago, I saw a man named Salvius. He took a blow meant for my uncle Forfar near his village to the north. When he died, his spirit came to me with the request to escort him to the Elysian Fields."

Ugard's eyes widened. "He came to you of his own accord and asked you to help him get to Elysium?"

Wiglaff nodded. "Yes, he did. And I asked him to take my hand. I took him where he wanted to go. His spirit is there now. I saw him there in my dreams."

Ugard asked, "You're sure his spirit came to you? And that he asked you explicitly to escort him to Elysium?"

"He said he understood I had escorted Festus to Elysium. He wanted me to take him there as well." Wiglaff stopped and twisted a thread of wolf's hide between his fingers.

Ugard asked, "How do you feel about granting his request?"

"Except that I am not a Roman priest, I felt relieved. It was the least I could do given the service both men gave my family. No one else could take them where they wanted to go. I was available. So why not?"

Ugard repeated, "Why not, indeed! Did you consider that the requests of these spirits were forms of a special calling for you?"

"Yes, I did, but I did not find them sufficient to answer the question you've posed. Besides, Elysium is a Roman idea.

The spirit of the butchered shaman was surprised I took him there ... and so were you, as I recall."

Ugard was speechless at this reminder. "The Greeks and Roman priests talked of a figure named Charon, a ferryman who pilots the spirits of the dead across the river of death to their final destination. We shamans are like that ferryman. We're not bound to a boat or a river, though. Our offices are for wandering spirits restless to get to a resting place."

Wiglaff said, "And I guess Elysium is as good a place as any." He continued to twist the wolf's leather in his hands. "Anyway, I'd better return to my meditations."

Ugard had one more thought. "The next time you see the girl in white, why don't you ask her what she portends for you?"

Wiglaff nodded. "I may just do that though the last time I tried to speak with her, she silenced me." Then he assumed his meditation posture on his bearskin and entered the land of living dreams. Ugard did the same, only with a different motive. His quest was to sort out the village wars to determine whether after the spring thaw the cavern would remain safe for their shamanistic activities.

***

The girl stood right in front of him, an emerald-green snake wrapped around her milk white arm. Her hair was braided, and her snow-white toga knotted below her waist. She was a virgin priestess, officiating at the altar of her god Mercury. Wiglaff was in her temple observing her conducting her rites. He ranged along with several enormously fat Roman senators and five wealthy knights. All the participants were more entranced with the priestess's beauty than with what she said to her god. Speaking in a stately, poetic rhythm, she was asking her god the answer to the questions she had received from the assembled men.

One Senator whispered to another, "Why don't we dispense with this nonsense? Let's escort this beautiful virgin to my estate and enjoy her charms."

The other Senator raised his finger to his lips. "Ruggius, don't blaspheme. Despoil the girl, and you'll have the Pontifex Maximus down on you like a hammer on an anvil. The knights need to hear her pitch. They'll donate fortunes for our purposes. You'll see."

Ruggius responded, "All well and good, but I still say we should enjoy her. Imagine a genuine virgin. Not even the Vestals are pure these days. This is not the Republic."

The priestess had a golden tongue that unlocked purses. The knights dropped their gold coins in the offertory as they left the temple. Ruggius patted the girl on her bottom as he left.

"Good girl!" he said under his breath. The priestess slapped his face hard, so the red imprint of her hand remained on his fat jowls. The other senator laughed so hard he had to cover his mouth.

Gasping for breath, he said, "Let's get back to the Senate. We have what we needed. Our special forces will have their new projectiles in time for the spring offensive in Caledonia."

The priestess was praying at the altar and weeping when Wiglaff found her. "Why are you weeping?" he asked her.

"No matter what I do, I am abused. My god does not protect me. One day a fat lecher like that Senator is going to take me right in front of the altar. I'll be ruined and banished from the clergy. I have no idea what I would have to do then to make a living."

"I'm not sure I can help you. Do you recognize me?"

"No, I don't. Are you going to rape me?"

"Not at all. I overheard one senator say the money you collected was to pay for special weapons to be used against the Caledonians."

She looked alarmed. "What happens to the money, I don't know. I'm only to make sure it keeps flowing into our coffers. I surely hope the money doesn't go for weapons as you say. I'm half Caledonian on my mother's side. My relatives would be at risk. My father is due to be rotated there in the spring. He's been promoted to Centurion. My mother hates it here in Rome. She can't wait to get home, but I'm afraid neither she nor I will be allowed north of the Wall. It isn't safe there. You look like a Caledonian. Do you think it's safe above the Wall?"

Wiglaff shook his head. "I think it's not safe for anyone north of the Wall. Once upon a time in a dream, I stood atop a high mountain where I looked out over all the world. Have you experienced a dream like that?"

She got a frightened look. "Are you a god?"

"I'm nothing of the kind. Don't be frightened. Will you answer my question?"

She said, "Yes, I've had that dream. My schoolmaster gave a lecture about the power and extent of Rome. That same night I had a vision where I saw everything all at once, from Caledonia to Asia. A figure stood on that mountain beside me. Was that you?"

"Yes. I was there. I tried to ask you a question, but you silenced me. Then I awakened, and you were gone." Wiglaff watched her eyes examining him from head to toe.

"I have to be going now. I'm sorry, but I didn't catch your name."

Wiglaff was about to tell the girl his name, but she vanished. He awakened sitting on his bearskin, no more informed, he thought, than when he entered his trance. Ugard was examining his face for signs of consciousness.

"I'm glad you've returned to the land of the living," Ugard told him. "You weren't breathing. I thought you might be exploring Elysium again."

"I think I should tell you what I've seen. Maybe together we can figure out what it means."

Wiglaff told Ugard about visiting the Temple of Mercury where the priestess in white worshiped her god. He told about the two senators and the five knights. He saw Ugard was alarmed about the use that was intended for the donations the knights had made. When Wiglaff finished his description, Ugard thought for a long while.

Ugard asked Wiglaff to repeat what he had said, slowly. He asked questions about each detail, including the snake and the incense. He even asked about the jewelry the senators were wearing. The name Ruggius was clearly repellant to him.

"You're sure they said the weapons would be delivered to troops in Caledonia in the spring."

"That's what the senator said. The question is whether the meaning was this spring or some other." Wiglaff thought through what he had seen, but he said, "I can't see the year of my vision."

Ugard said, "When I was in Rome, a great scandal broke out concerning defilement of the Vestals, who at one time had been sacred virgins, but now are openly used as political prostitutes though they're under protection as if they were still virgins, by the army and the religious community. A young rakehell named Ruggius, whose father was a senator … was at the center of the scandal. Apparently, he could not keep his hands off women, particularly virgins. I'm not certain, but I think your vision of the priestess takes place not in the present or the past, but in the future. How many years in the future it will occur, I can't say for sure, but I'll guess ten years. The advance warning gives us a little time. Did you ask the girl what you wanted to know?"

"Yes, of course," Wiglaff said, "but she surprised me. She didn't recognize me. She recalled having a figure like me by her side in a dream she had about viewing the whole empire from a mountaintop. Then she asked my name, and I woke up here."

"Apprentice, once again, you astound me. You went into your meditation seeking the spirit of a young girl. Instead, you observed the girl in her natural habitat, performing her normal function in the holiest of holies of her temple. You managed to gain knowledge not only about how Rome is siphoning money through the temples to fight their wars but also about how they intend to use special weapons against us Caledonians."

"Yet, Master, I am no further along determining my calling as a shaman." Wiglaff sounded crestfallen. His mentor commiserated for a few moments. Then he shook his whole body and spoke.

"I'm going to break all the rules and tell you what I think about your quest. You're still free to pursue answers however you like, but some things are crystal clear, at least to me."

Wiglaff was startled at the vehemence of Ugard's statement. He leaned forward and gave his mentor his full attention.

"Wiglaff, you might learn otherwise as you continue to meditate, but I have ample evidence that you have been called to become a shaman. Please indulge me while I tell you what I understand from your visions so far."

Wiglaff said, "Of course, Master."

Ugard held up his index finger and spoke, "First, you have been approached by a troubled spirit of a dead man. You did not approach the spirit, but the spirit came to you."

Wiglaff nodded. "That's true. Salvius's spirit came to me of his own accord."

Ugard smiled and held up his second finger and spoke, "Second, your spirit left your body and flew over the world, not just to fly over Britannia but to a place where you could view the whole world. Your spirit's flight is a major sign that you have been called as a shaman."

Wiglaff was now showing excitement in his posture and a sparkle in his eyes. The evidence was piling up in favor of his having been called.

Ugard now held up a third finger and continued, "Third, you have repeatedly been approached by a dream or spirit figure in the form of the priestess of Mercury. She appeared in many forms, all benign and some informative. The green snake she held is a more traditional form of such an approach, but it proves rather than reverses normal expectations. Definitively, this is a signal of a calling in that it's a manifestation of the very spirit who is calling you."

Ugard shook the three fingers in the air and smiled. Then he took down his hand and spoke slowly so Wiglaff could follow his logic. "Your attitude in your meditations shows a respect for the spirit world that goes beyond simple service. You tamed as well as tricked the butchered shaman. You dispelled the false spirits of the Romans and embraced the environment of the Roman afterlife. Your presence in the Roman temple indicated your ability to hold alien gods in respect if not adoration. Your doubts about your calling are exemplary in that you worried about every sign that your calling was false. In the end, you proved to yourself that every sign of your calling was true. And you proved to me that you deserve to be a shaman in your own right and my heir."

Wiglaff asked, "Master, where does this leave us?"

E. W. Farnsworth

Ugard laughed. "It leaves us exactly where we were before I launched into my explanation. You are still seeking, and I am still seeking answers, only now we have answered the most important question about your calling."

Wiglaff looked puzzled. "So what do we do?"

"Wiglaff, we do what shamans do. We meditate, we practice our rituals, and we do our offices for the spirits of the living and the dead in the world of vision and dreams. As for your unique gifts for divining the future and for gathering knowledge, those are secondary considerations, which will help Caledonia win the future contest with the Roman Empire."

Wiglaff cocked his head to one side and asked, "Does this mean that my insights are not the usual insights of a shaman?"

Ugard shook his head from side to side. "Wiglaff, what you are as a shaman differs from the norm as an eagle is different from a toad. You escorted a failed shaman to the Elysian Fields. He never could have arrived there by himself. Yet, in the end, he did not resent your taking him there. I've known shamans practicing throughout Caledonia who have none of your sense of calling or your skills at envisioning or your native intelligence. They are merely placeholders, complacent until they can't bring the rain anymore. They are meat for villagers' axes. Mark that you must never become fat and complacent. Your destiny is to stand apart and to be vigilant. To celebrate your new knowledge, I suggest we get some sleep. Winter won't last forever, so we must plan for spring."

Wiglaff had no trouble sleeping after his eventful day. He had followed all that Ugard explained about his calling. His mentor was persuasive and as eloquent as the young priestess of Mercury had been. Still, small vestiges of doubt remained in the young apprentice's mind, but he was confident he could now figure out his doubts without jeopardizing his growing sense of belonging. As Wiglaff fell asleep on his bearskin, he found himself on the mountaintop overlooking the world. A green snake was wrapping its body around his raised arm and grinning while flicking its forked, red tongue in and out of its mouth. His body wore only the loincloth made of stitched rabbit skins. He looked around but saw no figure of the maid of Mercury. Yet at his back whichever way he turned, he heard the distant whirring of tiny wings.

E. W. FARNSWORTH

E. W. Farnsworth lives and writes in Arizona. Over one hundred fifty of his short stories were published in a variety of venues from London to Hong Kong for the period 2014 through 2016.

Published in 2015 were his collected Arizona westerns *Desert Sun, Red Blood,* his global mystery/thriller about combating cryptocurrency crimes *Bitcoin Fandango,* his *John Fulghum Mysteries* about a hard-boiled Boston detective and *Engaging Rachel,* an Anderson romance/thriller, the latter two by Zimbell House Publishing.

Recently published by Zimbell House in 2016 were Farnsworth's *Pirate Tales, John Fulghum Mysteries, Volume II, Baro Xaimos: A Novel of the Gypsy Holocaust, The Black Marble Griffon and Other Disturbing Tales, Among Waterfowl and Other Entertainments and Fairy Tales & Other Fanciful Short Stories and The Wiglaff Tales, Book I of The Wiglaff Chronicles.*

Published by Audio Arcadia in England in 2016 were *DarkFire at the Edge of Time,* Farnsworth's collection of visionary science fiction stories, *Nightworld, The Black Arts* and *Black Secrets*. Farnsworth's *Desert Sun, Red Blood, Volume II, The Secret Adventures of Agents Salamander and Crow and Dead Cat Bounce,* an Inspector Allhoff novel, have been contracted for publication by Pro Se Productions, which will also publish his series of three *Al Katana* superhero novels in 2017 and 2018.

E. W. Farnsworth is now working on an epic poem, *The Voyage of the Spaceship Arcturus,* about the future of humankind when humans, avatars and artificial intelligence must work together to instantiate a second Eden after the Chaos Wars bring an end to life on Earth.

For updates, please see www.ewfarnsworth.com.

Book Two of the Wiglaff Chronicles

The Emergence
of the
Shaman

E. W. FARNSWORTH

1. According to *The Emergence of the Shaman*, what are the three key recognizable signs of the calling of a shaman? Do you agree with Ugard that Wiglaff finally satisfies all three of these signs? Do you think Wiglaff exceeds the traditional qualifications, or not?

2. What is the nature of the relationship between Ugard the shaman and Wiglaff the protégé? Is it static? Does it evolve? If the latter, discuss its evolution.

3. Why does Mordru think his son Wiglaff would not make a good warrior? Is he right?

4. Characterize the relationship between Wiglaff and his sister Winna from the points of view of (1) their father Mordru, (2) their mother Onna and (3) themselves.

5. Wiglaff's reclusive lifestyle befits a man who is destined to become a shaman. It also suits a man who is a natural spy. While the focus of these tales is the emergence of the shaman, how does Wiglaff's parallel emergence as a spy figure into the plot?

6. Bullies make life difficult for people who do not stand up to them. What becomes of bullies in these stories? Do they get what they deserve, or not?

7. The site of the historical Caledonian fort north of Hadrian's Wall is an object lesson for Mordru to teach his children. The location has a complex meaning for the plot. Elaborate on this idea and compare and contrast its purpose with that of the two Walls.

8. In the tales, how do the Roman intrusions on Caledonia affect relations between Rome and the Caledonians on the village level and on the level of the Caledonian Federation?

9.   The freed slaves Festus and Salvius are important for Wiglaff's personal development but in different ways. Compare and contrast their service to Wiglaff's extended family as well as their contributions to Wiglaff's discovery of his inherent shamanistic skills.

10.   When he returns to Wiglaff's village in the south, Mordru wants to hear the story of Festus's journey to the distant sea from him and not from Winna. Yet Winna protected Festus during the trip. Is she right to feel neglected? Is she vindicated in the end?

11.   Freia, the wild child, is among many women who enter Wiglaff's life. Compare her with his sister Winna and with the unnamed priestess of the god Mercury. What is Freia's opinion of the status of her relationship with Wiglaff when they part?

12.   Wiglaff becomes a student of all things Roman, including language, customs, and military strategy. Ugard also has long experience with Rome and Romans. On the other hand, Mordru eschews the study of Roman culture on the grounds of security. Do you think an intelligent Caledonian should have ignored learning about the culture of the people who are bent on conquering them? Why or why not?

13.   Shamans are born; they are not made. Attack this idea with reference to the method of Ugard's shamanistic teachings.

14.   Festus is both a scholar and a warrior. In this respect, he is a lot like Wiglaff. How far does this comparison extend?

15.   Rome's corruption is everywhere apparent in these tales. Do you think America in our own times is more

or less corrupt than ancient Rome was? While you discuss this, consider whether the American Empire today is or is not a mirror of the Roman Empire at its greatest extent. Explore military, political, cultural, religious and economic perspectives.

16. Women warriors are developed clandestinely to combat the military power of Rome. Why must their presence be protected as a closely held secret, even in Caledonia?

Other Works by E. W. Farnsworth

John Fulghum Mysteries

John Fulghum Mysteries Vol. II

John Fulghum Mysteries Vol. III-Blue is for Murder

Engaging Rachel

Pirate Tales

Baro Xaimos: A Novel of the Gypsy Holocaust

Fairy Tales and Other Fanciful Short Stories

Among Water Fowl and Other Entertainments

The Black Marble Griffon & Other Disturbing Tales

Book One of the Wiglaff Chronicles: The Wiglaff Tales

Coming Soon from E. W. Farnsworth

John Fulghum Mysteries, Vol. IV: The Perfect Teacher

John Fulghum Mysteries, Vol. V: Finding Harry Diamond

A Note from the Publisher

Dear Reader,

Thank you for reading E. W. Farnsworth's second book in
The Wiglaff Chronicles: The Emergence of the Shaman.
We feel the best way to show appreciation for an author is by
leaving a review. You may do so on our website:

www.ZimbellHousePublishing.com, Goodreads.com,
Amazon.com, or Kindle.com.

We hope you enjoyed this novel.